GREENMONKEYGAMEBOOKS

PRESENTS

TROPIC TERROR

A PICK YOUR PATH ADVENTURE

Also by Matt Beighton

The Shadowland Chronicles
The Spyglass And The Cherry Tree
The Shadowed Eye

Monstacademy Series
(Ages 7+)
The Halloween Parade
The Egyptian Treasure
The Grand High Monster
The Machu Picchu Mystery
The Magic Knight

Pick Your Path Series
Escape From Sherwood
Desolate Tomb
Beast of London
The Fall Of District-U
Tropic Terror

buy them all from mattbeighton.co.uk/shop

HUGE THANKS TO ADAM, JASON, JULIAN AND LOUISE WHO
MADE SURE THAT THIS BLASTED THING WORKS!

I COULDN'T HAVE DONE IT WITHOUT YOU ALL.

THE ZOMBIES ARE COMING...

TROPIC TERROR

Copyright © Matt Beighton 2024

Matt Beighton has asserted his right under the Copyright, Designs and Patents Act, 1988, to be identified as the author of this work.

Printed in the United Kingdom

First printed 2024

A CIP catalogue record for this book is available from the British Library.

ISBN: 978-1-915814-01-2

illustrated by Darwin Setiawan

cover illustration by Darwin Setiawan

www.mattbeighton.co.uk

www.pickyourpathadventures.com

My mama always told me someday I'd be good at something. Who'd a' guessed that something'd be zombie-killing?

- "Tallahassee", Zombieland

INTRODUCTION

This is an adventure with a difference. You control the direction that the story takes. It is possible, with a few wise choices, to navigate the book with minimal risk. However, most adventurers will find that they encounter a host of pitfalls and monsters throughout their journey. How you handle these events will have consequences further on in the story. Choose wisely, and watch where you step.

A WORD ON DICE

Throughout the book, you will see references to the use of dice. Unless it clearly states otherwise, you should use a standard six-sided die (D6). Some points reference 2D6, this simply means roll two dice and add the result.

CREATING YOUR CHARACTER

Before you begin your adventure, you need to generate some characteristics for your character. These are your **HEALTH** and your **STRENGTH**. These will be vital throughout your adventure. Your health will change throughout, whereas your **STRENGTH** will only change with potions or weapons.

To generate your **HEALTH**, roll 2D6 and add 6 to the total. This is your original **HEALTH**. No matter what potions you find, your **HEALTH** can never go above this number.

To generate your **STRENGTH**, roll 1 die. Add 6 to the total. This is your original **STRENGTH**. Certain potions and weapons can increase your **STRENGTH** above this number for a short period.

FIGHTING BATTLES

When you are faced with a battle, you must defeat the enemy to move forwards in the story.

First, record the enemy's **STRENGTH** and health on your **BATTLE SHEET**.

1. Roll both dice and add the total to your **STRENGTH**. For instance, if you roll a 3 and a 5 and your **STRENGTH** is 9, your attack is 3 + 5 + 9 = 17. Now do the same thing but add the **STRENGTH** of your foe.
2. If the scores are the same, roll again for both of you.
3. Whoever has the highest score wins this round of the battle. Remove **2 HEALTH POINTS** from the loser.
4. If you are using a special weapon, remove **1 DURABILITY** point.

If you have any ALLIES, fight for them now, repeating steps 1-4 for each ALLY.

5. Repeat steps 1-4 until the health of either you or your enemy reaches zero.

6. When one of the health scores reaches zero, the battle is over. If your health has dropped to zero, you have been killed, and your adventure is over.

TESTING YOUR STRENGTH

At various points in your adventure, you may be required to test your STRENGTH. This is a way of testing whether you are strong enough to complete a certain action. To test your STRENGTH, roll two dice and add the scores together. If the number is less than your current STRENGTH, you are successful. If the score is the same as or higher than your current STRENGTH, you are unsuccessful. You must follow the instructions each time, depending on what you roll.

POTIONS AND ELIXIRS

During your adventure, you may be given potions or elixirs. These have positive effects on your health and STRENGTH. Unless they say otherwise, HEALTH POTIONS only restore your health to your original level. Therefore, it is important to use them wisely. **STRENGTH POTIONS** increase your **STRENGTH** temporarily. Once you have completed an action or finished a battle, your **STRENGTH** returns to its original level.

Some potions restore your health fully. Others only restore a certain amount of points. These will be indicated with brackets in the name: for example, a **HEALTH POTION (+4)** will restore **4 HEALTH POINTS**. It is even more important to use these wisely. If you use a **+4 HEALTH POTION** when you are only 2 points below your maximum, you will only benefit from +2 points. The other two are wasted.

WEAPONS

Various weapons are scattered throughout the adventure. Unfortunately, they are all well-used and won't last for very long. Each weapon has a **DURABILITY**. This tells you how many rounds of battle it will last. **Note**: this isn't how many full battles, but how many individual rounds. Therefore, it is very important to use special weapons sparingly. If you are up against a weaker enemy, it's probably best to stick with your hands or something that you don't mind running out. You can use special weapons for single rounds if you prefer; maybe you need to deliver a killer blow during a particularly close fight and only want to use 1 durability point on a weapon.

You start the adventure with nothing but your bare hands. They don't run out (obviously) but they don't have any special effects. This is to fall back on when you have no other weapons.

Some weapons may have dual effects. For instance, a **BLADE OF DEFENCE** will offer some protection during a fight and mean you only lose **1 HEALTH POINT** per round that you lose. However, it is also very heavy and means you take a **-2 STRENGTH** hit. Remember, these benefits and negatives only affect you during rounds where you use that particular weapon. Your **STRENGTH** returns to normal when you use another weapon.

Various weapons may have **KEYWORDS** associated with them. If they do, make a note of them as they may give you extra benefits in certain situation.

If you run out of **WEAPON** slots, you must drop a weapon before you can take another.

Unless specified, **ALLIES** fight using their fists.

ALLIES

At certain points in your adventure, you may meet others who wish to join your cause. These are classed as **ALLIES**, and you will be told when you may add them to this list. **ALLIES** are a great way to boost your fighting capabilities. After you have rolled for yourself and your enemy, you get to do the same thing again for each of your **ALLIES**. Your enemy fights them as they do you, so if you have one ally, the enemy could do two lots of damage (one to you and one to the ally).

When you meet **ALLIES**, you will be given their **STRENGTH** and **HEALTH** to record on your **BATTLE SHEET**. Sometimes, you will be asked to generate one or both of these scores. Instructions on how to do this will be given each time.

If, at any point, an **ALLY'S HEALTH** drops to zero, that **ALLY** dies and cannot be used again. You may use any potions that you possess on an **ALLY**, but remember to remove them from your **PACK** when you do. You cannot split potions. Likewise, any weapons that you possess may be used by your allies. Remember to keep track of how many times they are used, the same as if you were using them yourself.

If your own health drops to zero, your adventure is over regardless of how many **ALLIES** you have. You cannot continue your quest as an **ALLY**.

You may have multiple **ALLIES** at once.

ERRATA

Fixes for any known issues can be found at mattbeighton.co.uk/errata

INFECTION

INFECTION is a real and present danger on an island filled with zombies. You have a natural **IMMUNITY**, which you need to generate at the start of your adventure. Roll 2D6 and add the numbers together. This is your starting **IMMUNITY**. Every time you are wounded by an **INFECTED** animal or any type of zombie, deduct 1 **IMMUNITY** point as well as your **HEALTH**. If it doesn't say otherwise, assume any enemies are **INFECTED**.

Once you run out of **IMMUNITY** points, you are considered to be **INFECTED**. The only way to cure an infection is with a **FIRST-AID KIT**. Once you are **INFECTED**, you must test your **STRENGTH** every time you start a new section in the book. If you fail, you loose a single **STRENGTH** point. Once your **STRENGTH** reaches 0, you are too weak to continue.

A **FIRST-AID KIT** will restore your **HEALTH** and cure **INFECTION**, but any lost **STRENGTH** points are gone for good.

RANDOM ENCOUNTERS

Throughout your time on Ghost Island, keep an eye out for this symbol:

This means that you have entered a **RANDOM ZOMBIE ENCOUNTER** zone. Roll a die and consult the table at the back of the book to see which fiendish foes you have to slay to continue on your adventure. Roll a second die and half the result, rounding up (you can also roll a D3 if you have one to hand). So if you roll a 5, you halve it to 2.5 and round up to 3.

This tells you how many you need to fight (unless you encounter an **ABHORRENT GHOUL**).

BACKGROUND

The heavy grey storm clouds that have hung over the aquamarine ocean slowly disappear as you draw closer to the island. You can see the soft bar of sand in the distance, but the course that the skipper is taking zigzags you back and forth across the waves. It draws closer slowly, and the incessant chatter of the others on the boat grates against your nerves. You are aching to feel the soft sand under your feet and a cold drink in your hand. After all, that's what these conferences are all about.

Not that you'd ever admit that to anybody back home. MediCorp Conferences are well known amongst the peddlers of pharmaceuticals that you mingle with, and not just for the exciting new medicines that often premiere at these things. There are rumours that there is something spectacular this year, but nobody can tell you exactly what it might be.

The setting for this year's MedCon is even more intriguing. The idea of a tropical getaway is nothing new, but Ghost Island is so remote that it doesn't appear on many maps. Your flight took you into the Maldivian capital of Malé before a two-day cruise took you away from civilisation.

You landed in a small port on another anonymous island before being transferred to the speed boat that is now finally bringing you to your destination. All of that for a three-day conference seems excessive, but if the new medicine is that impressive, then it makes sense.

The rest of the people on the boat are a strange mix of sales, advertising and science. You can tell those in sales and advertising by their stories of one-upmanship and the fact that they've hit the on-board margaritas hard. The scientists are sat on the edge of the boat, looking nervous and isolated. You move over towards the one who seems most likely to talk.

You introduce yourself to the woman, perhaps in her forties and dressed in a pair of combat shorts and a t-shirt advertising an unknown rock band. She doesn't say much, not even her name. You push her for more information, and she gets up to leave, obviously finding the pressure uncomfortable. As she does, she turns and fixes you with a piercing glare. "You're here now. We all are. It doesn't matter why. It's Henrik Flagstaff, the big deal. It'll be a big deal, alright. Bigger than anything you've ever seen. You'll soon see. Just remember, earthquakes are big, too. It doesn't make them good."

With her ominous words nestling in your ears, you move back to the other side of the boat and take a seat next to your small suitcase. The weather is forecast to be hot and humid, so you've packed light. You sit back and watch the rest of the scientists for any signs of what's to come, but they give nothing away, and soon, the boat grinds to a halt against a long wooden pier.

"Off you get," the captain grumbles, not leaving his post. "If you need picking up, you'll have to send a message from the comms unit in the tourism centre. Good luck."

Another portentous message does nothing to calm your nerves, but you seem to be the only one who's listening. The sales and advertising executives are already staggering down the wooden platform towards the beach and inevitable bar, whilst the scientists are hovering towards the back of the boat, gathering up their luggage.

You put your paranoia down to jet lag and drag your case over the lip of the boat and onto the pier. The wood is dry and brushed with salt. Reed-covered parasols

cast welcome shade every couple of
feet, but the heat in the open is already
unbearable, and there are still a few hours
until nightfall. Parrots squawk overhead,
swooping through the air until they come
to rest in the coconut palms that punctuate
the island. Even from here, you can see
the tall visitor centre in the middle of the
island and a lookout point in the distance.
It would surely take less than an hour to
cover every square meter on foot, but the
layout of wooden buildings, swimming pools
and trees gives the illusion of a much bigger
paradise.

"They shouldn't be here," somebody says,
approaching you from behind. You turn
and smile at the same scientist that you
approached on the boat. "Every living thing
on Ghost Island was brought here for this
resort. Nothing belongs here. We certainly
don't."

"What do you mean?" you ask.

She shrugs and picks up her small case. "It
doesn't matter. Forget I said anything. Just
be careful and look after yourself."

Before you can respond, she picks up the
pace and heads into the treeline at the end
of the pier. You follow as quickly as possible,

joining the line of conference attendees snaking out of the glass doors of the tourism centre.

These things never go smoothly, and by the time you reach the check-in desk, they inform you that they have overbooked the resort and you will be sharing a room with one of the other guests. They make it clear that they have upgraded you to a deluxe, ocean-view hut at the rear of the island, but you still leave in a foul mood. When you arrive at your hut, you are dismayed to see that your new roommate has already passed out asleep on the couch. The sleeping situation isn't as terrible as you feared – the hut is divided into a living area and two separate bedrooms, each with its own bathroom. Perhaps this won't be so bad after all.

You throw your case into the larger of the two rooms and change into something more comfortable. A clock, designed in a garish and false tiki style, ticks over to six o'clock. Time for the welcome meeting and a chance to see just who you are stuck here with and what is going on. You make your way to the business centre and take a seat near the back of the auditorium.

YOUR CHARACTER'S NAME:

Starting strength:
Current strength:

Starting health:
Current health:

Starting immunity:
Current immunity:

WEAPONS:

Weapon:
Strength effect:
Durability:
Notes:

Weapon:
Strength effect:
Durability:
Notes:

Weapon:
Strength effect:
Durability:
Notes:

Weapon:
Strength effect:
Durability:
Notes:

Weapon:
Strength effect:
Durability:
Notes:

Weapon:
Strength effect:
Durability:
Notes:

ALLIES:

Name:
Strength:
Health:
Notes:

Name:
Strength:
Health:
Notes:

Name:
Strength:
Health:
Notes:

Name:
Strength:
Health:
Notes:

Name:
Strength:
Health:
Notes:

Name:
Strength:
Health:
Notes:

BATTLES:

Enemy: Strength: Health:	Enemy: Strength: Health:	Enemy: Strength: Health:
Enemy: Strength: Health:	Enemy: Strength: Health:	Enemy: Strength: Health:
Enemy: Strength: Health:	Enemy: Strength: Health:	Enemy: Strength: Health:
Enemy: Strength: Health:	Enemy: Strength: Health:	Enemy: Strength: Health:

YOUR PACK:

You open your eyes and groan. A thunderbolt splits your vision, your throat feels dry, and your eyes are swollen and sore. You grope around until you are satisfied that you are in your bed in your hut. Vague memories of the previous night lap against the shores of your memory, but none are clearer than a faded watercolour. What little you can remember seems hectic and filled with screams and terror.

A weak crack of light stabs through the curtains, casting a glow over the hideous tiki clock. It's just after six in the morning. It's far too early to be awake, especially feeling as rough as you do.

Slowly, you try to piece together the night. You know that you didn't have a drink, but your body feels like you put it through the ringer. Every joint aches, and your eyes water when you roll over and sit up on the edge of the mattress. Through the open doorway in the living area of your hut, you can still hear the low snores of your new roommate.

Unusually, there are no other sounds.
You've stayed on tropical islands before,
and the wildlife usually do all they can to
wake you up with their cries, but this one is
silent. The scientist on the boat mentioned
that none of the wildlife was native;
perhaps they are kept locked away at night,
like in a zoo?

You vaguely remember sitting down to
watch the first speaker of the night, but
he was timid, and his voice barely reached
the back of the auditorium on the ground
floor of the business centre. You tried
your hardest to keep up with the notes
on his slideshow, but they were far too
complex, wandering through the tangled
history of tissue regeneration and bacterial
recomposition. You got the gist that they
had somehow found a way to regrow
damaged or necrotic tissue, but beyond
that, nothing.

The rest of your memories are a little hazier.
Every time you try to think past the man's
speech, it is clouded in a thick fog.

You stand up and throw on a set of clothes,
making a note of the heat that is already

permeating through the walls. You sling a
backpack over your shoulders and decide to
set out to explore the island to learn more
about what happened.

To head into the living quarters, turn to **224**.

To take a bit more time looking through
your room, turn to **188**.

2

The padlock splinters under your final
strike, and the door slowly creaks open
enough for you to wedge your fingers past
the edge and pull it open. A stale stench
wafts from the space beyond, filling your
nostrils with hints of rotten meat and
grease.

It takes your eyes a moment to adjust to
the dusty darkness in the room beyond,
and you take care not to walk into anything.
You keep one ear open for the sounds of
anything moving about, but there seems to
be no sign of life.

Turn to **164**.

3

As you approach the gazebo, you realise that it has been decorated for a wedding. White bunting is hanging from the rafters, and tiki torches and rose petals adorn the walkway. From this distance, it's hard to make out more, but there appears to be the silhouette of two people moving on the gazebo itself.

To continue forward, turn to **204**.

To head back, turn to **184**.

4

The room is a chaotic mess with bedding and clothing strewn across the floor and hanging from every surface. Whoever was staying in here left in a hurry. There isn't anything of real value to you, but you notice a small black notebook on the bedside table. You grab it and read the first few pages, making a note that it is a diary, clearly from somebody working at the event last night. A loud thump against the wall startles you, and you decide to make a hasty exit. Add the **DIARY** to your **PACK.**

You rush out of the door and back into the corridor. To explore the rest of the passageway, turn to **129**.

To head back downstairs, turn to **182**.

5

The rest of the room turns up nothing much of interest, although you do find a **FIRST-AID KIT** to add to your **PACK**.

FIRST-AID KIT:
Restores health to maximum and cures **INFECTION**.

If you'd like to reconsider searching the corpse, turn to **127**.

Otherwise, you can leave the building by turning to **14**.

6

It doesn't take long before you emerge at a wide plaza. There is a large swimming pool off to one side, surrounded by sun loungers and wooden huts. A sign overhead tells you that it boasts a poolside bar. Ahead, the path continues down towards the beach.

To your right, a barked path winds its way towards the entrance to the tourism centre.

To investigate the pool area, turn to **190**.

To head towards the beach, turn to **88**.

To follow the path to the tourism centre, turn to **231**.

7

Shunning your sense of impending doom like a tattered robe, you stride forward. You cast the light of your torch in every direction, hoping to catch the edge of something or a sense of where you might be heading. All the while, an overwhelming weight of darkness settles on you, crushing the light from your eyes. Within seconds, you are lost in the darkness. You spin around, but there are no markers from where you came, no purple glow or shards of crystal. You desperately grope in the darkness, blind to everything but your own hopelessness. In a way, it is a welcome release when you stumble too far in one direction, and the ground disappears beneath your feet, casting you tumbling into an unending pit. You seem to fall forever, the expected crash never coming. When it does, it is a blessing, releasing you from your fears and the pain of the living.

8

Rounding a corner, you find yourself at the foot of another set of steps. You climb them to reach an open area of stone at the top. Cracked and split by some unknown earthly force, the stone base is cold to the touch. You explore it thoroughly but find little of interest other than a few mushrooms, each one embedded with purple crystals.

If you wish to pick a mushroom to add to your **PACK,** turn to **101**.

Otherwise, you may return to the path and continue through the caves. Turn to **143**.

9

In desperation, you scan the horizon for any sign of a ship, but there is nothing but aquamarine for miles in every direction. For a moment, you consider diving into the water to escape the oncoming horde, but then you notice that the zombies who didn't make it onto the jetty are circling beneath you, treading water and waiting for your arrival.

You pull out your weapons and make short work of the first zombies to arrive, but there are more, always more. No matter what you do, they are piling up behind each other, desperate to get into the fray. The stench and heat from their bodies is unbearable, and you begin to feel faint. In a way, passing out would be the kindest way to go, unaware of the savage mauling that your body is certain to be subjected to.

They don't grant you that favour, scrambling over one another until your body is crushed beneath their mass. Teeth and nails scratch and tear at your skin, your heart racing as it fights against the virus coursing through your body. Within seconds, you succumb, darkness sneaking in from the sides of your vision until all is black and peaceful.

10

The growling increases in pitch and volume as you approach, and you quickly realise that the dog isn't just injured; it is infected. It isn't just one dog, either. As

you approach, the rest of the pack appears from between the trees. Before you can react, the dog on the steps lunges at you. The others hold back for now, but it doesn't relieve the immediate pressure. You manage to swat away the first attack, but it is on you again quickly. Subtract -2 from your first attack roll against the **INFECTED DOG**.

INFECTED DOG:

Strength: 13
Health: 16

If you manage to put the beast out of its misery, the rest of the pack flees for now. You know that if you return this way again, they will be back. Taking advantage of their absence, you consider your next step. To push on through the doors of the tourism centre and into the open reception area. Turn to **52**. Alternatively, you can continue along the path past the building. Turn to **25**.

11

The man on the other end of the line seems to be considering this for a second before his voice crackles back through. "Call the coastguard. Rescuing sailors is their thing."

Choose your response:

"I'm not a sailor! I'm stranded on the island but had to escape, so I swam out to the boat." Turn to **207**.

"I tried calling them, but they didn't pick up." Turn to **89**.

12

You turn on the torch and are immediately bathed in a weak yellow light. It doesn't reach far into the cave, but it is enough to help you find your way. You think back to your days spelunking with friends through caves back home, but none of them was as dark or foreboding as this one.

After a while, you start to notice a pale purple glow emanating from the stones in front of you. Soon, it is bright enough that you can turn off the torch and still see. You push on, ducking under low ceilings and admiring vaulting passageways, until you finally emerge at a set of roughly-hewn stone steps. They lead down into a vast cavern, bathed in the purple light of crystals protruding from the walls. In the distance, you can just about make out a rope bridge crossing a still lake and, beyond that, a pathway that appears to rise out of the caves.

You clamber down the steps and reach a split in the path. You can't see much in either direction at this level.

To turn left, turn to **8**.

To carry on ahead, turn to **143**.

13

"You're hardly a castaway there. There are daily boats for tourists, so I suggest you contact the boat that took you there and see when they are going to collect you. You can reach them on **CHANNEL 37**. Good day."

With that, the radio clicks off, and despite your efforts, you are unable to reach the airfield again. Eventually, the battery dies, and you give up. Turn to **173**.

14

You decide to leave through the back door, but as you are leaving the room, a side door bursts open, and a whirling ball of angry energy steams towards you. At first, you

are convinced it is another zombie ready to devour you, but after a second glance, you realise that the person is alive but just as angry.

"You're one of them!" she screams, wielding a baseball bat and swinging it towards your head. She is dressed in a skirt and blazer, and the name badge on her chest marks her as Fern.

She seems hell-bent on taking you out, but you have a brief window to try to talk her around. If you'd sooner ignore that and attack her back, turn to **156**.

To try to engage her in conversation, turn to **128**.

15

Once you are past the horde of zombies, the smell dissipates along with your nausea. Here, the path splits in two. One track leads past the front of the business centre. You can head that way by turning to **40**. A few yards away, there is another track that seems to lead towards the tourism centre. To follow that track, turn to **65**.

16

The hut is crowded with piles of clothes
and dirty plates. Whoever has been living
here recently has been here for a while.
You hear movement at the back of the hut,
possibly from the bathroom, but something
else catches your eye. On the table, there
is a black metal box marked with the word
FLARE. To open the box, turn to **17**. To leave it
where it is and retreat from the hut, turn to
117.

17

You open the box carefully, wary of what
might be inside. The lid flips back easily,
and you find a **FLARE GUN** nestled in a bed of
foam. You may add it to your **WEAPONS** if you
choose.

FLARE GUN:
Strength: +5
Durability: 1

As you turn to leave, you realise that
whatever was making the noise is now in
the room with you, blocking off your exit.

Roll for a **RANDOM ZOMBIE ENCOUNTER.**

If you survive, turn to **117**.

18

You shuffle into the room, trying your hardest not to make a sound. Roll two dice. If you roll a double, turn to **30**. Otherwise, turn to **157**.

19

"Sorry, pal," the captain says, shoving you in your chest. "Nobody gets a free ride." The others have started to pile in now, with mob rule taking over. You glance back and see the frenzied swarm waiting for you back on the dock. Before you can beg for another chance, the captain pushes you again, sending you sprawling back into the water.

You surface in time to see the boat slowly moving away and the swarm of swimming zombies closing in. You fight back as well as you can, but they are too strong. Eventually, they clamber on top of you, forcing you underwater. Your ears ring with the pressure, and your lungs burn. The pain is quickly replaced by the salty taste of water gushing into your mouth.

By the time you surface again, your strength is gone, and the zombies attack.

You put up precious little fight as they begin to feast on any flesh they can find, thankful only that your death will be quick.

20

It doesn't take you long to reach the end of the beach, where it is cut off by a row of rocks that thrust out into the ocean. From here, you can clearly see the wreck, and it looks to be genuine. Unfortunately, there are no boats to take you out to it, so your only option will be to swim. It is too far to swim unaided, so you will need the correct equipment.

If you have **SCUBA EQUIPMENT** in your **PACK**, turn to **57**.

Otherwise, there is no way for you to reach the boat, and your only option is to return back along the beach towards the caves. Turn to **223**.

21

You know that the **KEY CARD** opens something in the tourism centre, so you decide that might be a place to head towards. Checking that nothing is following you, you head back along the boardwalk until you reach the fork in the path. One direction heads back towards the business centre, which you rule out. The other leads straight on, so you head that way. Turn to **201**.

22

Without fins, it is hard work to force your body to the bottom of the ocean, but you manage it within a minute or so. Taking care not to damage the coral, you use the shards of rock to pull yourself towards the chest. You are disappointed to find that the reflective items it contains are not, as you hoped, gold coins, but a handful of aluminium cans that have obviously drifted there in the current.

Turning back to the boat, you feel something heavy hit you in the back. You spin around, lashing out with your feet, but there is nothing there. The bottom of the hull is nothing more than a gaping hole here, and it's hard to keep your eyes on every direction.

Panic rises through you, making you take deeper breaths. Conscious of how much

oxygen you might need to return, you try to calm yourself down, but just as you start to breathe more normally, you are struck again.

This time, your attacker doesn't disappear. You turn to see the bulk of a large shark heading away from you before it performs a tight turn and begins to accelerate towards you.

Like the remnants of the humans on the island, the virus seems to have infected the shark. As it hurtles towards you, you notice a trail of blood behind it, seeping from a wide-open wound in its belly. Its intestines are hanging out, flapping in the water like a flag. Its face is a patchwork of scars and suppurating sores, its mouth missing most of its lips.

If you have a **SPEAR GUN,** turn to **133**.

Otherwise, turn to **147**.

23

You admire the well-manicured gardens that line each side of the pathway. Towering palms are interspersed with tall, red

flowers that reach out to touch your legs.
At another time, it would be a paradise
to spend your time here, but now every
shadow seems to hold a new terror. Parrots
whistle and screech overhead; even the odd
monkey scurries through the branches of
the occasional mango or creeping fig tree.
Before long, you reach a small hut clad in
wooden strips and topped with thatch. A
bright pink sign, chipped and hanging from
a single chain, reveals it as "Tom's Tiki
Treats", a cocktail bar for the patrons of the
resort.

If you would like to dig around inside the
hut, turn to **76**.

To carry on along the path, turn to **237**.

24

The mast is barely wider than your waist,
so you will need all of your balance to make
it to the other side. You decide to sit down
and straddle it instead of walking across. It
slows you down but makes balancing easier.
It still isn't easy work. Every movement
causes the mast to roll sideways, throwing
you with a sickening lurch to the other side.

The gulf between the two halves of the boat is roughly fifty metres, and each one is a splinter-inducing pain in the backside. You push on until you are over halfway before you dare to glance down. Beneath you, the dark yawning maw of the ocean seems to be rising up to swallow you. You try to look away, but a sickening dizziness grips you until you are barely able to maintain your grip on the wood.

Test your **STRENGTH.**

If you pass, turn to **189**.

If you fail, turn to **66**.

25

As the path winds away from the tourism centre, you relish the peace that seems to be falling. It is fast approaching midday and the sun is high and hot in the sky, but the air is silent other than the sizzle of insects in the bushes. You slow your pace and take your time considering your next move. The beach is to your left, beyond a tightly packed grove of trees. The path you are on seems to curve towards it further on. However, you notice a narrow passage to your right, packed with rough gravel but well-maintained. It seems to cut through to another pool on the other side.

To continue onwards, turn to **99**.

To cut through the bushes, turn to **177**.

26

The final hut is set back from the path with a wider front porch area. A tray of half-finished drinks has been left on a table, and a bowl of fruit is slowly decaying in the heat. To check inside, turn to **97**. To walk past, turn to **81**.

27

"I work better alone," you mutter. "Besides, it'll be easier to run away from people if there's only one of us to worry about."

You don't wait to see the look of hurt on his face. You push past him and head to the door. Turn to **80**.

28

You begin to panic, desperately cursing yourself for your failure. If you have a **KEY CARD**, turn to **46**. If not, turn to **9**.

The room beyond the double doors is large and harrowing. The air still tastes acrid, although the white mist has long disappeared. Rows of blue chairs spread out like a spider's web, some thrown backwards, others still standing. Some of them are still occupied by silent corpses. They must not have survived whatever happened.

"Help." The voice betrays its owner's weakness and vulnerability, but you can't work out where it is coming from. "Please."

You move around the room, tossing chairs out of the way. When you reach the stage, you hear the voice again, louder this time but still barely audible. You lift the fabric skirt at the front of the stage and step back. A young woman is curled up in the foetal position, rocking slightly and holding one hand against an open wound on her arm.

"Help," she repeats.

You take her other hand and slowly help her out of her hiding place, supporting her over to one of the chairs where she sits.

"My name's Hannah," she offers. You shake her proffered hand. "I feel responsible for all of this." Her sweeping arm takes in the room.

"You caused all of this? All of that out there?" you ask.

She shakes her head. "No, not really. But I didn't stop it. It was Henrik Flagstaff."

Suddenly, another memory barges its way into your brain. You remember Flagstaff from last night; he was the big deal everybody was hoping to see. The scientist on the boat mentioned something about him-

"You were on the boat," you say, remembering the woman's face. "We spoke."

She nods. "I tried to warn you. I warned everybody. I couldn't get him stopped, though. I knew it would be bad, but I had to come to try to get him to reconsider."

"What happened?" you ask.

"He had a new virus to demonstrate. He promised that it would be a new biological

weapon that armies around the world would fight for. He wasn't wrong."

"It escaped?"

She shakes her head. "Worse, he let it loose. I don't know the full details; you'll have to have a poke around, but somebody here must have known what was going to happen. We just have to hope that they recorded it somewhere."

You thank Hannah for her help and ask her if she'd like to join you. She winces and shakes her head again. "I'm injured. I'll be alright, but I need to sort myself out and get to safety. If you find a way off the island, send help for the rest of us. There are probably more survivors out there."

Hannah stands up and wanders off to tend to her injuries. You head back out through the double doors. If you haven't explored upstairs yet and would like to, turn to **175**.

Otherwise, you leave the centre behind and head back to the path. Turn to **116**.

You approach carefully, making sure to keep to the shadows in the dimly lit kitchen. You navigate your way through metal trolleys and scattered pans without making a sound. As you draw closer, you realise with horror that the chef is undead. His left eye darts back and forth across his rotting ingredients, whilst his right is nothing but an empty socket. His chef's hat and apron are speckled with dark patches of mould, but the most disturbing thing of all is the food he is preparing on a silver platter. The eyeless head of a young man, severed from his body and drained of blood, is nestled amongst a pile of decaying vegetables. As you watch, the chef stuffs a maggot-riddled apple into his mouth.

Retching, you reach out until your hand closes around a chopping knife. You lunge forward, bringing it around in a neat arc, taking the zombie's head clean off.

You flee the scene and head back into the serving area up front.

Turn to **44**.

"Just leave me alone," the man cries.

You perch on one of the stones and ask him his name and why he is here. He introduces himself as Herbert. "I came here when the resort first opened. I discovered these caves and decided that this was where my future lay. You know, rich people used to pay hermits to live in caves on their land? I thought I could be the island's hermit, and people would pay me to live here."

"And do they?" you ask.

Herbert shakes his head. "That there is the crux and nubbin of it. Nobody actually knows that I'm here. It's a tragedy, really. But, it does mean that I get to see everything that goes on here."

You sense that he might be useful after all. "So, you know what happened last night? What caused the zombies?"

Herbert looks sheepish. "Well, you see, I tend to know everything that's going on more, sort of, after it's finished happening. Information takes a while to reach me, what with me being underground and nobody coming to see me and all."

Exasperated, you push him for more information. "Do you know anything?"

Herbert seems to disappear inside himself for a moment as he thinks, but suddenly, his eyes light up. "I did venture out this morning for some breakfast." At this, he gesticulates to a leather shoe roasting slowly over a small fire. "A few of them attacked me and I managed to give them a good kicking."

"But, you don't have a weapon. How did you manage that?"

Herbert taps his nose and winks. "It's easy, really." He leans in and whispers something in your ear. You laugh at the simplicity of it. "Don't tell anybody else," he warns you, "otherwise Herbert will add you to his collection." With a laugh, he points at the row of skulls resting on a flat piece of rock. Most of them look like cheap Halloween decorations, but a few look disturbingly realistic.

Thanking him for his help, you stand up to

leave. From now on, you know **HERBERT'S SECRET.** Whenever you fight any type of **ZOMBIE,** reduce its listed **STRENGTH** by 4.

Returning to the path, you may explore the dark tunnel by turning to **141**. Otherwise, head to the rock face by turning to **146**.

32

You enter an open area of grass, bordered with scented flowers and tall candles. Most of them have been knocked to the ground, rather spoiling the Zen atmosphere. Several yoga mats have been scattered across the opening, possibly by the group of zombies squabbling in the middle of the circle. All of them are dressed in the same attire: brightly-coloured leggings and loose-fitting t-shirts. Whatever benefits yoga gave them in life, it has made very little difference to their post-infection appearance - their skin is sloughing to the ground even as they wrestle in front of you and their muscles, once toned and supple, hang in ribbons from blistered wounds.

Whilst you stand and take in the scene, your arrival hasn't gone unnoticed. One of

their heads snaps back, and the creature
locks eyes with you. It howls, and the
others pick up the mournful wail.

You back away quickly, tripping over a piece
of machinery concealed by the bushes.
You pull yourself to your feet using its
handle and realise it is a petrol-powered
lawnmower. A thought creeps through your
brain as the ravenous horde gathers around
you. You shake yourself free of all other
weapons and take hold of the mower. With
a sharp tug on the line, the engine roars
to life, and you step into the middle of the
arena, imagining yourself a gladiator about
to take on the heroes of Rome.

One by one, the zombies throw themselves
at you. You raise the lawnmower, swinging
it over your head and in wide, sweeping
arcs around your waist. When it connects
with a body, the fierce blades shred the
undead flesh, sending it spiralling off into
the bushes. Soon, there is only a handful
left.

Roll a die. You must fight that many
zombies with the following stats:

YOGA ZOMBIES:

Strength: 15
Health: 12

Your only weapon is the **LAWNMOWER.**

LAWNMOWER:

Strength: +5
Durability: Until the yoga horde moves no
more

Once you are satisfied that the zombies
are nothing more than shredded meat,
you gather up your weapons, reluctantly
accepting that the lawnmower is not a
suitable weapon to take with you, and head
back out to the path. Turn to **225**.

33

Outside the restaurant, the air is humid
and hot. You take a moment to recover
and catch your breath, but stay alert for
any attackers. You are on a wooden deck
bordered by a waist-high rope fence. There
is a small swimming pool in front of you,
the water murky with blood. To your left,
the deck ends at a set of steps that lead
down to a crazy-paved pathway. To your

right, it joins with another sand pathway
that seems to branch off in three directions.

To head left, turn to **102**.

To head to the right, turn to **124**.

34

You thank Fern for her offer but explain that
you prefer to work alone. She seems hurt
and scared and begs you to reconsider.

To do so, turn to **41**.

To stand firm, turn to **180**.

35

When you are satisfied that you are alone,
you explore the perimeter of the roof, trying
to work out what to do next. The heat up
here is unbearable; every moment tightens
your headache's grip and dries out your
mouth and skin.

If you have summoned a **HELICOPTER,** turn to
82.

Otherwise, turn to **159**.

Immediately, you get the sense that you are following the path into a staff-only area. The landscaping is bare here, and there are piles of old crates and other detritus lined up along the edge of the path. Eventually, you reach the back of the tourism centre. Air conditioning units and rusting pipework hang from the wall like odd metal monkeys, and the strange clicks of insects fill the air. There is a single door set into the wall, metal with a small glass window. Metal bars on the other side prevent you from smashing it to gain entry, and the door is held closed by a sturdy lock. You can try to smash it with a weapon if you choose. You may attempt it as many times as you like, but each attempt removes **1 DURABILITY** for the weapon that you use.

Roll two dice and add them to your **STRENGTH** as though you are attacking an enemy. If your total is 14 or greater, you smash the lock and enter the building. Turn to **75**.

If you can't smash the lock or wish to walk away, turn to **183**.

37

The radio crackles to life, hissing and spluttering, but there is definitely a weak voice on the other end. You move the dial slightly, trying to clear the static, and suddenly, a strong female voice booms through. She swears at something on her end before returning to the matter at hand, introducing herself as the captain of the Azure Queen. You recognise the name; it was the boat that dropped you off yesterday. You try to explain that you need an emergency evacuation, but the captain seems uncertain. She asks you why.

To tell her the truth, turn to **230**.

To lie and tell her that somebody is seriously injured, turn to **70**.

38

The door is seized shut, the hinges rusted in place by years of neglect. An old, heavy padlock links together a chain wrapped around the handle. The only way through is to use a weapon of some sort. If you have collected a weapon, you may use it to break open the door, but it will take three strikes to do so. If you use it, remove 3 from its **DURABILITY** and turn to **2**. If you don't have a weapon or decide to walk away, you can return to the path by turning to **145**.

39

Opening the glass doors, you are hit with the powerful scent of a thousand tropical flowers drifting in on the damp breeze. Even with the doors open, the air is almost silent. You can hear the soft susurration of the sea washing over the sand in the distant cove and a strange groaning sound that puts you in mind of a broken-down air conditioning unit clinging to life.

The balcony is wooden, with a low handrail surrounding it. There is a small gate on one side that leads to a dirt path down the hill towards the cove.

To investigate the path, turn to **135**.

To return to your living quarters, turn to **224**.

40

The path is blocked by a staff-only gate, but it has been propped open by a boulder. You push through, kicking the stone clear, and recoil as the gate snaps shut behind you. A magnetic bolt slides back into place, locking it. Your only way forward lies ahead of you.

After a few meters, you reach the entrance to the business centre. The events of last night are still a blur in your mind, but if anywhere holds the answers, it is inside that building. The door to the business centre is propped open with a chair, but the lights inside are turned off. It would be easy to enter to see if you can find any answers about last night, but there is also a strange tension in the air. To enter the building, turn to **112**. To ignore the business centre and return to the track, turn to **116**.

41

Thanking you profusely, Fern promises that she will be useful.

"Listen," she says, offering you a small plastic card, "take this. If we get separated, it might come in useful."

You accept her **KEY CARD** and add it to your **PACK**.

Add **FERN** to your **ALLIES**.

FERN:

Strength: 14
Health: 18
Immunity: 9
Special: Fern is extremely loyal. If a blow would kill you, Fern will dive in front of the attack and take the hit, losing **2 HEALTH POINTS** herself. She will do this until she dies herself.

Once you have sorted everything out, you head out of the building and rejoin the path. Turn to **202**.

42

The boy drops to the floor in a twitching mess of muscle and flesh in perfect unison, with the doors sliding open to reveal the reception area. You step clear of the elevator and into the marbled space. Turn to **195**.

43

The elevator rises swiftly and soon reaches
its destination at the top of the building.
The doors slide open slowly, revealing an
open expanse of hot concrete. You rush
out eagerly, forgetting to check what is out
there and stumble straight into a horde of
zombies.

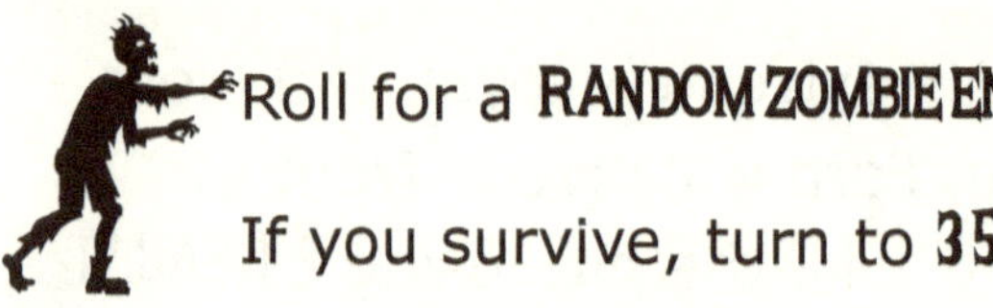

Roll for a **RANDOM ZOMBIE ENCOUNTER.**

If you survive, turn to **35**.

44

You stay put for a few minutes to recover
from what you have just seen. As you idly
play with the items under the counter, you
discover a couple of **FIRST-AID KITS.** Add both to
your **PACK.**

FIRST-AID KIT:

Restores health to maximum and
cures **INFECTION.**

If you haven't investigated the shed yet and
would like to, turn to **220**.

Otherwise, turn to **162**.

With a guttural roar, the man falls from the jetty into the sea, staining it red. You stagger to your feet, broken and weary but alive. Your nerves sing with paranoia, desperately keeping your focus on the jetty, searching for more attackers. Even as the captain swings the Azure Queen into the dock, killing the engine and letting the boat glide into the wood with a soft bump, you feel uneasy.

The captain lays a wooden plank across the gap, connecting the boat to the jetty, and you offer heartfelt thanks. As you place a foot onto the bridge, the captain stands up and raises a hand. "Stop," she warns. "I know what went on here. Those things," she points at the corpses lining the boards, "are infectious. I need to know, are you infected?"

You have no choice but to answer honestly. You may take this opportunity to cure any infection if you have the resources, but the captain doesn't look like the type of person to suffer fools.

If you are **INFECTED,** turn to **107**.
Otherwise, turn to **167**.

46

Your fingers grip the card, and your hopes lift slightly. Perhaps you have a final chance to secure passage off this island. You can't wait around for more of the virus-riddled zombies to find you, so you head back along the boardwalk. When you reach a fork in the path, you weigh up your options. You recognise that one direction will lead you back towards the business centre, which seems a waste of time. The other leads straight ahead towards the tourism centre, so you head that way. Turn to **201**.

47

"I don't like your snarky attitude," the man on the other end of the line seems angry. "If you need my help, you might want to think about talking to me with a bit more honesty."

"You're right, I'm sorry. It's been a long day, and I'm afraid for my life. Please, come and help me." Turn to **170**.

"Forget that. This place is crawling with zombies! I need you here now!" Turn to **227**.

48

There is barely a sound in the air as you walk through the vegetation, basking in the humidity and the heat. Sure enough, the path soon forks, heading south towards another pool and north towards a beach.

To head south, turn to **94**.

To head north, turn to **187**.

49

You pull the flare gun from your **PACK** and fire it high into the sky. Despite the bright sunlight, the trail of red smoke is clearly visible, and you notice a change in activity on the boat. Optimistic that they will realise that somebody on the island needs help, you throw the flare gun aside and head back along the track.

You have successfully summoned a **PARTY BOAT.**

Whoever is on the boat is unlikely to wait for long when they reach the dock. If you aren't there to greet them, you know with a sickening certainty that they will return to their party on the waves.

From this point, you are racing against the clock. If you are using the character sheet at the front of the book, use the egg timer icons to track your progress. If not, keep track on a piece of paper. Each time you turn to a new section, you must mark off a timer, each one representing one minute. If you do not reach the party boat within ten minutes, you risk being trapped on the island.

You hurry back along the path until you reach the main junction next to the burning barrel. To follow the first track, turn to **40**. To head along the second track, turn to **65**.

50

"Emilia?" you ask, remembering the couple on the beach.

She looks at you, shocked. "How did you know?"

You explain about her parents and how they were protecting themselves on the beach to the north of the island. Emilia leaps forward again, giving you another hug. "Thank you!" she looks lost for a second before continuing, "I need to go to them. I'm sorry,

I wanted to help you, but I need to see my parents."

Nodding in agreement, you offer a hand for her to shake, trying desperately to avoid another hug. Then, something occurs to you. You rummage in your **PACK** until you find the **MOBILE PHONE** and hand it to her. Emilia quickly turns it on and unlocks it. "I can tell them to meet us here!" she exclaims, quickly dialling a number.

You wait patiently whilst she explains where you are and persuades her parents to come to you. "They weren't at the beach, anyway," she says after hanging up. "They're only outside the tourism centre, so they won't be long."

You settle down again to wait. If you're honest, the rest is welcome, and you can feel it doing your body the world of good. By the time Emilia's parents knock on the door to the shed, your **HEALTH**, and that of your allies, has been restored to its maximum. The two older tourists agree to tag along, so you may add them to your allies.

"This is Pam and Horatio," Emilia says, introducing her parents.

PAM:

Strength: 9
Health: 14
Immunity: 2D6
Occupation: Personal Trainer

HORATIO:

Strength: 8
Health: 10
Immunity: 2D6
Occupation: Retired Landscape Gardener
Special: Horatio is armed with a set of gardening shears that he has picked up somewhere. They deal out 3 points of **HEALTH** damage each time instead of the usual 2.

Once introductions have been made, you leave the shed. Turn to **149**.

51

Once you are out of the shadows of the business centre, the trees thin out, and you emerge onto a narrow sandy track at the top of a rocky precipice. The track winds along the coast of the island, the sea crashing against rocks perhaps twenty feet below. Every so often, you dip back into the cover of towering trees. Here, coconut palms have given way to stouter trees with branching canopies that form dark tunnels.

It's only when you emerge blinking from one of these that you realise you have stumbled onto another pack of rabid zombies. They are just as startled by your arrival as you are by them. Deduct 1 from the number of enemies that you must face.

Roll for a **RANDOM ZOMBIE ENCOUNTER.**

Once you have slain your enemies, turn to **158**.

52

The reception area is filled with white marble that reflects the harsh sunlight in disconcerting ways. You blink in the brightness and explore the area quickly. Your footsteps ring out and echo off the walls, threatening to alert trouble with each step. You try not to move too much, glancing around you from where you are. There isn't much, but you do find a FIRST-

AID KIT behind the main reception desk. Add it to your **PACK.**

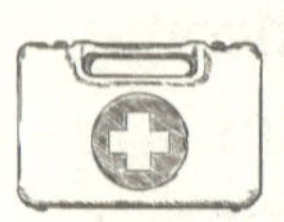

FIRST-AID KIT: Restores health to maximum and cures **INFECTION.**

Other than that, you can see a set of elevator doors marked for the roof of the building and a set of stairs that appear to lead down into a basement.

To enter the elevator, turn to **43**.

To descend the steps, turn to **200**.

53

You kick the final rat's body into the corner of the room and open the only door. It leads out into a communal area. Turn to **171**.

54

Your foot crashes into the door, splintering the lock and sending it banging back against the wall. You check for any signs that the noise has attracted attention before entering the building. Turn to **171**.

There is an acrid smell inside the hut, a mixture of cheap body spray and sweat. You push on, keen to see if there is anybody else here who might help you fill in the blanks from last night.

Whoever was staying here isn't here now, and they don't seem to have packed much to bring with them. You step over a few pairs of gaudy swimming shorts and vest tops with offensive slogans before finding a large **FIRST-AID** kit shoved behind the sofa. You add it to your **PACK.**

FIRST-AID KIT:

Restores health to maximum and cures **INFECTION.**

You turn at the sound of something brushing against the rear wall of the hut. It sounds like it is coming from outside, but you can't be sure. You strain your ears, but you don't hear it again. To continue investigating, turn to **191**. Otherwise, if you'd rather leave, turn to **83**.

56

The groaning of the bridge is still portentous, but it seems to hold your weight. You grab the side ropes and propel yourself forward as quickly as you dare. Beneath you, the water froths with ravenous fish, eager for a meal that they desperately need. You make it to the other side without incident and finally breathe a sigh of relief as you step onto the hard stone again.

The path splits three ways. Ahead, it seems to dip down into a small "room" of sorts carved out by erosion. To the left, it rises towards a dark tunnel. To your right, the path seems to terminate at a rock face, although the rocks seem easily climbable from your position.

To turn left, turn to **141**.

To head into the "room", turn to **213**.

To head to the rock face, turn to **146**.

The tight rubber seal around the snorkel mask pinches the edges of your eyes but feels secure enough. You twist the valve on the small oxygen tank and place the mouthpiece between your teeth. A few swift inhalations and you are satisfied that it will get you out to the boat. Whether there will be enough oxygen to get you back is another question, but you put it to the back of your mind. After stripping down to your underwear and placing your clothes in a neat pile behind a rock, you wade out into the water.

Despite the seemingly endless sun, the water has a welcome chill to it, soothing your skin and giving you a jolt of energy. The ocean bed slowly drops away until you are perhaps a dozen meters from the shore, and then it suddenly disappears. You splutter to the surface, sort out the oxygen tank, and dive underwater.

Beneath you, an aquamarine world stretches away in every direction. The white sand of the ocean bed is decorated with brightly jewelled fish that dart amongst the rocks and coral. Ahead of you, the hulking mass of the boat seems within touching distance, a strange effect of the light.

Swimming forward, you take in everything, trying to keep your bearings straight at all times. You are maybe a few meters from the boat when you notice something that looks remarkably like a wooden chest filled with a strange item reflecting the beams of sunlight. It is nestled on the sand amongst towering stacks of coral but should be easy enough to reach.

Resting your hand against the hull of the boat, you see a series of wooden pegs that form a ladder up onto the deck.

To swim down to the chest, turn to **22**.

To climb the ladder, turn to **144**.

58

You turn right, squeezing your body around the bend. You quickly discover that the shafts of light are coming from small holes in the ceiling of the tunnel, but they aren't big enough to poke through. The tunnel itself continues ahead towards the humming sound that is gradually getting louder. There isn't enough space to turn around, so you continue forwards.

Turn to **118**.

59

There is no space to move through the trees, and the branches scratch your legs and face. Roots seem to rise out of the ground, determined to trip you, but you stumble forward, swatting spiders' webs from your face. Eventually, you step into one too large to swipe away, so you retreat a foot or so and consider another way around. As you do, an enormous spider, larger than your face, appears on the web. Whatever virus has infected the people on the island also seems to have

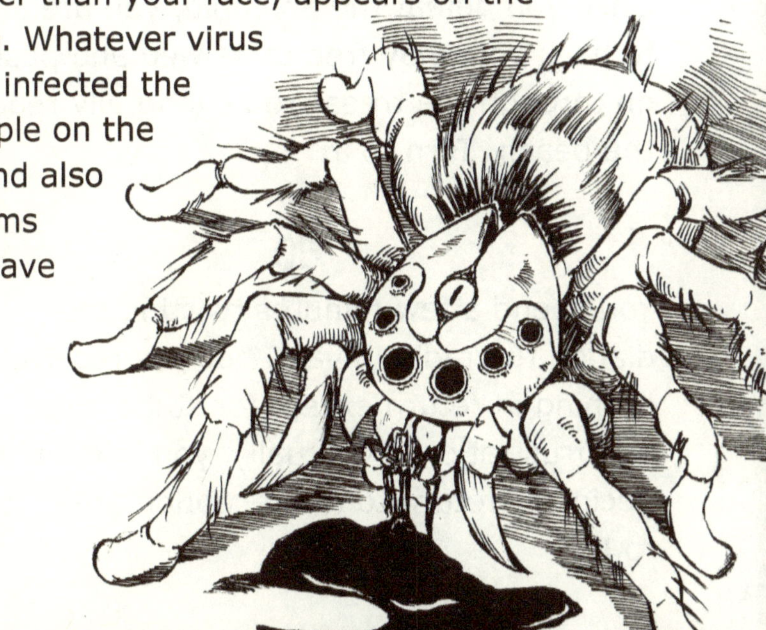

reached the spider; its black fur is patchy, replaced by pale skin and puss-filled blisters. Its many eyes swivel to focus on you, each one piercing red and oozing. Its mandibles clatter and drip with venom, each droplet smoking when it lands on a leaf.

You consider retreating, but it's too late. When you walked into its web, several strands must have attached to your waist, and there is no way to quickly pull away. Instead, you are forced to fight the beast.

MUTATED TARANTULA:
Strength: 12
Health: 12

Once you defeat the arachnid, you are able to hack your way free of its web and push on through the trees. You eventually reach the beach. Turn to **91**.

60

You spend a few minutes twisting the dial on the radio in vain, but you receive nothing in return except for static noise and frustration. Eventually, you give up and decide to return to the reception area. Turn to **113**

Considering your options, you realise that your best option is to return to the business centre and retrace your steps. You leave the dock and head back along the path until you reach the entrance to the business centre.

If you have explored the business centre before, you may return to the path and begin retracing your steps. Turn to **116**.

If you would prefer to investigate the business centre, turn to **112**.

62

You rummage through the remaining items on the gazebo and discover a **PISTOL** tucked into the waistband of a resort security guard. It has seen better days, but it will allow you to get off a few quick shots in a bind. Add it to your **WEAPONS**.

PISTOL:
Strength: NA
Durability: 5

Special: You can fire the PISTOL at any point during a fight. If you do, don't roll any dice for you and your enemy. Instead, you automatically cause 1 **HEALTH POINT** damage.

When you are satisfied that there is nothing else for you here, you head back to the beach and turn towards the dock where you arrived yesterday. Turn to **184**.

63

Your first impressions were correct, and the main body of the stern is entirely empty. However, when you glance over the edge on the far side, you notice a small wooden rowing boat strapped to the hull. It takes you a few minutes, but you are eventually able to haul it up onto the deck. It appears to be watertight, and the oars seem sturdy enough.

If you are ready to leave the ship, turn to **148**.

If you haven't tried to reach the bow yet and wish to do so, turn to **24**.

64

You explain everything that you know so far to Elrond. He looks bemused at first but finally lets out a large sigh. "I'm glad

I missed it," he says. "There was loads of noise just after midnight. It woke me up. You weren't back, but it sounded like people were fighting and shouting outside."

"That could have been when it all started," you say, trying desperately to piece everything together. What did you see last night? What happened? Why were you fine, other than a grinding headache?

You notice a hopeful look in Elrond's eyes. "It might not be safe out there alone," he says. Before you can react, he reaches behind a cushion on the sofa and withdraws a large, curved sword. "From the gift shop!" he cries, giving it a few experimental swings. One nearly takes your ear off, but it definitely seems sharp. "I was a radio engineer in the army if that helps."

You understand what Elrond is asking.

If you would like to take him, turn to **172**.

If you'd sooner head out alone, turn to **27**.

65

This close to the centre of the island, there is a strange calm. Here and there, you hear the screams of zombies or possibly even survivors, but it is mostly silent. The tourism centre, a block of glass that looks like an iceberg stranded in the middle of the island, towers over you, silent and dead. Some lights are still on, a remnant of the haste that overtook everything last night, but there is no movement. The entrance is towards the south side of the island, ahead of you.

You follow the pathway, taking your time to check the shadows for zombies. You feel something wet hit the back of your neck and turn your head, but there is nothing there. You put it down to water dripping from the palm fronds that form an umbrella overhead, but when your neck starts to burn with a fierce intensity, you stop and look around.

Suddenly, another droplet of liquid hits your arm and then another on your cheek. Both begin to burn almost immediately with a pain that is only dulled when you wipe the liquid away with your shirt.

It occurs to you to back away, but whatever is attacking you remains hidden. You turn back to face the path, and your enemy finally reveals itself. An ant the size of a small dog steps out from the undergrowth. It leaves a trail of smoking green bile wherever it walks. You duck just in time as another globule of acid erupts from its mouthparts and is ejected towards you. You knew there were FIRE ANTS on the island, but this one is larger than any insect you've ever seen. It is quick and dodges your attacks easily, spitting acid at you whenever it gets the opportunity. Instead of rolling two dice to add to your strength, you may only roll one for this battle.

GIANT FIRE ANT:

Strength: 9

Health: 6

If you vanquish the insect, you return to the path. Turn to **6**.

66

You try desperately to grip the mast, but your fingers have no strength left in them, and your arms feel weak. You slide sideways, throwing your body forward and wrapping your arms tightly around the wood. Closing your eyes, you try to block out the sense of space beneath you as you slide free of your perch, only your feeble arms holding you above the water.

There's no point in calling out; nobody would hear you, so you remain silent and contemplate your own foolishness. When your arms predictably fail in their task, and you plummet into the dark water below, it's almost a relief to accept your fate. You thrash about for a while, trying to find your way to the hull of the boat.

Roll a single die.

If you roll an odd number, turn to **131**.

Otherwise, turn to **85**.

67

Together, you find space amongst the gardening tools to sit and rest. As you listen, she tells you about how she ended up here.

"I was here with my parents," she explains. "We were staying in the holiday rentals just over there." She points towards the gate opposite the shed. "We were attacked last night, just after midnight. I don't know what happened."

If you think you know the girl's name, turn to **50**.

Otherwise, turn to **168**.

68

The ground underneath your feet is soft but solid enough to walk easily on. It rises slowly as you progress until you are once again high above the cavern below. It seems to be filled with smaller "rooms" almost, where the paths intersect or where water has eroded the walls. In one of them, you are sure that you can see a semi-naked man dancing around. There is no time for that now, as the path has brought you back to the world outside. Shafts of sunlight streaming through an opening herald your return, and you clamber clear and step back out onto the island. Turn to **120**.

69

You follow the corridor until it emerges into a wider area lined entirely with concrete and filled with old cardboard boxes. You begin to move some of them out of the way but stagger back when a pile of them erupt with noise and violence.

Roll for a **RANDOM ZOMBIE ENCOUNTER.**

If you survive, turn to **196**.

70

"I don't have the medical expertise or the speed to get anybody to a hospital quickly," she says urgently. "You'll need to contact the coastguard or the water ambulance service on the mainland. They'll be able to get your patient to safety more quickly."

With that, the radio cuts off. You try desperately to regain contact, but she is gone. Without her help, there is no way for you to leave the island. You search for a phone to call the coast guard or water ambulance, but the lines are dead. You decide to try again later, but for now, you are stuck and abandoned by cruel fate.

Even as you wait, holed up in a small comms room, you hear the sounds of zombies breaking down the doors outside. It won't be long before they reach you and put you out of your misery. You will no doubt put up a valiant defence, but your fate is sealed. This island will become your tomb.

71

To head south, past the pool and towards the beach, turn to **88**.

To follow the path round towards the tourism centre, turn to **231**.

72

You settle back on one of the benches and begin to enjoy the feel of the wind against your burned skin. After a few moments, the weight of sleep drags your eyes closed, and you relinquish consciousness. Your dreams are dark, filled with savagery and an unending lust for something that you can't quite sate. You wake with a strange terror gripping your heart and dampness around your mouth. When you open your eyes, everything is pale, as though seen through an old movie. The ship is in chaos; people are screaming and crying out at you.

You look down, finally noticing what is in

your hands. It is an arm, one that was once attached to the captain. Looking at the damage you have dealt to the rest of his body, he is beyond needing it. In your sleep, your infection has taken over; turning you into one of the monsters you fought against. Somewhere deep inside you, you can feel the last vestiges of humanity shrivel and die, replaced only by an insatiable thirst for flesh.

The rest of the party-goers offer little resistance to your madness, and soon, yours is the only soul on board if, indeed, you still have one. The wait ahead of you will be long, but you know that there will be plenty to quench your bloodlust when you arrive on the mainland. Instead of helping to prevent the spread of the virus, you have become the very vector that you sought to avoid. The curse of Tropic Terror isn't over for you. It never will be.

73

You edge closer, trying to close your nose to the foul smell coming from the pool. Even from here, you can see that the water is far from clean. You dread to think what foulness has putrefied it since last night, but that is the least of your worries.

Upon closer inspection, the body in the chair appears to be deceased. Caught in two minds, you decide that the humane thing to do is make sure that they are beyond help, so you step closer still. From here, you can see that they are dressed in a vivid Hawaiian shirt and beach-party attire; they've even got a surfboard propped up against their chair.

The suddenness with which the body reacts to your intrusion startles you, sending you backwards until you step into the shallow water of the pool's edge. It feels uncomfortably thick as it oozes over your foot. The zombie rises to its feet, the terrifying appearance of its ghoulish features somewhat offset by the fact that it has picked up its surfboard to attack you with.

It waddles towards you, its arms flailing and getting tangled in its gaping body. If you retreat any further, you will be forced to swim across the pool to the other side, which seems to be a shortcut through to

the beach. You may escape that way at any
point in the fight by turning to **142**.

SNAZZILY-DRESSED TROPICAL ZOMBIE:
Strength: 12
Health: 13

If you stick around for long enough to send
the zombie to the great beach party in the
sky, you may leave by swimming to the
far side of the pool as above, or you may
return to the path and head towards the
tourism centre by turning to **138**.

74

Just as you approach the edge of the
dock, and the horde of zombies seems to
be bearing down on you with imminent
destruction in mind, you notice the party
boat appear round the headland. Refusing
to waste another second, you leap from the
jetty and feel the embrace of the cold water
engulf you. When you surface, a couple
of flailing zombies who have joined you in
the water make a half-hearted attempt to
attack, but you push them away and swim
towards the boat. It slows down enough to
allow you to climb aboard at the stern, and

you hurriedly tell the captain to take you as far away from shore as possible.

Before he does, he insists that you pay your way. "This isn't a free taxi," he complains.

One of the other partygoers steps forward and chips in, "Nobody gets on board without bringing something for the party!" The others cheer their approval.

If you have anything suitable for a party, turn to **165**.

Otherwise, turn to **19**.

75

You enter the building on the basement floor, into a long corridor lined with concrete walls and a damp, concrete floor. Broken lights buzz at odd intervals, casting a pulsing disco glare that begins to give you a headache. Turn to **69**.

76

The hut is small and cramped. The three walls opposite the serving hatch are taken up with shelves stacked with alcohol and a large metallic ice machine. You clamber through the hatch and move the bottles around until you find what you are looking for. You take the strong alcohol and a dry piece of cloth, ramming the latter into the neck of the former. Grasping the neck of the bottle, you get a feel for the weight of your Molotov cocktail, a fearsome weapon that might just come in handy.

MOLOTOV COCKTAIL:

Strength: -
Durability: 1

Special: Nothing can survive the raging inferno created by this crude weapon. It must be used in the first attack against an enemy. When you use it, test your **STRENGTH.** If you are successful, it strikes any and all enemies that you are currently fighting, killing them. If you fail, your weak throw misses them, and the moment is wasted.

You add it to your **PACK** and climb back out of the hut. Continue along the path by turning to **237**.

77

The approach to the hut is shrouded in the shadows of palm trees, giving you a brief respite from the sun. You push the door open and step inside, recoiling immediately from the stench. Whoever was renting this space didn't make it out of bed alive, although as you watch, their unalive corpses slowly start to stretch and rise to greet the day. They shuffle towards you slowly, their matching silk pyjamas torn and hanging from their broken bodies.

SLEEPY ZOMBIE #1:

Strength: 10
Health: 15

SLEEPY ZOMBIE #2:

Strength: 11
Health: 11

If you defeat them both, turn to **153**.

78

You follow the short path until you arrive at a small hut, topped with a grass roof and adorned with a chipped chalkboard sign introducing "WetZone Watersports Rentals". The side door appears to be hanging open.

To head inside, turn to **111**.
To head back to the crossroads, turn to **226**.

79

The door creaks but doesn't give way. There is no way you are going to open it with your weak body, so you continue to look for other ways in. Further along the building and higher up on the wall, you notice an air vent. By standing on one of the rotten benches, you can just about reach up and pull the grating free. It crashes to the ground, and you wince at the thought of attracting attention.

Using every ounce of strength, you are able to pull yourself up and into the vent, fighting against the claustrophobic sense of everything closing in. You control your breathing and begin to shuffle forward, sliding on your stomach and trying hard not to scrape it where the metal joins.

Turn to **229**.

80

Before you leave, Elrond grabs your arm. "I wasn't completely honest," he says. He looks embarrassed, but you can't work out why. "I have a bit of an idea about what's going on out there."

"What do you mean?" you ask.

"When I heard the noises last night, I sat at the window watching for a while. It looked like a zombie apocalypse. They were everywhere, attacking each other and anybody else they could get their hands on. I don't know if they really are zombies or if it's some sort of virus, but they certainly acted like them."

You take a moment to let this sink in. "Lots of them?"

Elrond nods. "Dozens. Some of them were stronger than others, and some seemed more intelligent. I don't know why. I tried to work it all out last night, but it was all a bit much."

You thank him for sharing his information before heading out of the door.

The air is sizzling already, promising yet another day of dry and overwhelming heat. You blink in the bright, reflected light and try to get your bearings. You didn't have much time to pay attention when you arrived yesterday, and you still have no idea what happened later on. There is a broad sand path running past your hut, leading to the right, where it appears to reach a dead-end after a few more huts, and to the left, where it curves away through a manicured avenue of trees.

To turn right, turn to **210**.

To turn left, turn to **145**.

81

You continue past several other huts, all darkened and with locked doors. Eventually, you hear the sound of the ocean on the other side of the trees and pick up your pace. As the path straightens out, you find yourself approaching a metal gate that appears to be locked. Turn to **217**.

82

You wait on the roof for a few minutes before you hear the welcome hum of helicopter rotors in the distance. It doesn't take long to reach the roof, where it settles onto the concrete like an oversized bird returning to its nest. A man waves you

towards him just as the elevator doors ping again, releasing a fresh horde of attackers. You see the man's eyes widen, and a sense of relief washes over you. At least he will believe you weren't lying!

The zombies are too busy fighting each other to get through the doors to pay you much attention, and you make it across the roof to the rear doors of the helicopter in time to see them descend into a huddled mass of violence. As you rise into the sky, grateful to finally be free, you reflect on what has happened.

If you have a **DIARY** in your possession, then you know everything about what happened and are able to rest easily, knowing that the authorities will be well-equipped to deal with the consequences.

If not, then your freedom is the only thing that you have won. The secrets of what transpired on the island will remain a mystery until somebody braver than yourself is able to return and unpick the mess. Take solace in your safety, but know that it is a hollow victory.

83

You leave the hut, gulping down mouthfuls of the fresh tropical air. To check out the back of the building, turn to **38**. To return to your own hut and head along the path in the opposite direction, turn to **145**.

84

You explain what you saw in the forest on your way to the beach. The two survivors look horrified.

"It was eating somebody else?" the woman asks. The man throws up violently, making sure to aim it outside of the barricade. A look of terror swims across her face. "It wasn't a young woman, was it? About 19 years old? Brown hair, a tattoo on her left arm?"

You think back to the victim and shake your head. "No, it was a man. Who is the girl?"

"Our daughter," the man adds. "We were separated. We have no idea what has happened to her. If you see her, can you give her this?" He throws a **MOBILE PHONE** to you. It is locked but has a full battery. You turn it off quickly and add it to your **PACK.** "Can these things be killed?"

You nod and tell them about its attack and how you managed to kill it with a stick through its chest.

"Thank you for your information," the woman shouts. "But, we've not got space in here. We need to keep a space for Emilia. You need to find your own place to hide."

Just as you are about to turn and leave, the man calls out to you. "Take this," he yells, tossing the RIFLE down onto the sand. A couple of boxes of ammunition follow. "We've got a couple in here, and you'll definitely need it out there."

"Whatever happened to them all last night, it seems to have affected a lot of them. The whole area was swarming with them this morning. Some of them were lightning-quick, others slower but seemed stronger. Be careful out there."

Thanking them both, you add the rifle to your **PACK.**

RIFLE:
Strength: -
Durability: 12
Special: Whenever you start a fight, you

may fire one round at your enemy before they engage you. This automatically deals out **2 HEALTH POINTS** damage to them without the need to roll any dice.

Just as you turn to leave, the man shouts after you again. "You may as well have these." He tosses a small wooden box down to you. It is a box of **FIREWORKS.** You add them to your **PACK.**

"You never know. You might find a party out there!" he finishes with a weak laugh. You thank him for his generosity. There are no other ways out of the cove, so you head back along the path towards your hut. After climbing back onto the balcony, you head for the living area. Turn to **224**.

85

After endless thrashing in the water, the water begins to fill with dark shadows. Just as you fear that the hunters of the ocean are about to strike, your back bumps up against a wooden plank. You grab hold of it and manage to pull yourself clear of the water. It quickly becomes apparent that it is a set of wooden stairs, rotten but serviceable, that lead back up to the front of the boat. Staggered at your own fortune, you scramble up them and reach your destination. Turn to **236**.

86

The next passage is written on a scrap of paper in scrawled handwriting, hinting at the urgency of the author.

This is probably the last thing I'll get to write, but I need to get my thoughts down on paper. Henrik Flagstaff turned up full of bravado and arrogance. He refused to temper his speech and was determined to show the full power of his new virus. To that end, he deployed several canisters at the front of the stage that were designed to release the virus over the front row at a certain point. His plan was to show how they began to change, how their personalities would leave them and render them nothing more than mutants and zombies. He assured us that he wouldn't let it go too far before releasing the second canisters that contained the vaccine.

"It will be nothing more than a hypnotist's trick," he roared with his enormous voice. "They might have a few bad memories, but for everybody else, it will be a hoot!"

I still don't know what happened. From where I was standing at the back, it looked like one of the canisters was facing the wrong way, and it filled the stage with smoke as well as the front of the audience. Henrik inhaled his own poison. He wasn't able to release the vaccine. The damage was done.

I managed to escape along with a few of the others sitting towards the back, but I think we all inhaled some of the white fog. I woke with the worst headache this morning, but thankfully, that seems to be the only side-effect.

If I'm right, then the vaccine is still there in the canisters in that room. If we can get a message to the authorities, it might not be too late to reverse this tragedy.

That seems to be the end of the author's notes. Fern is crying softly, but she seems determined to carry out the last request in the note. Turn to **197**.

87

You explain that you are as unclear on what happened as she is but that you hope you can find out together. Slowly, she begins to come around, and she asks if she can join you.

To accept Fern's offer, turn to **41**.

To reject it, turn to **34**.

88

As you pass the pool, you pick up on
some strange sounds coming from the
area. You're sure you can hear somebody
whistling, but it might also be the last
desperate groans of the undead. You ignore
it and push on until you reach a bend in the
track. Turn to **203**.

89

"What do you mean? They aren't a
restaurant. Call the damn coastguard."
The radio goes silent. You swivel the dial
and scream into the microphone until
the battery dies, along with your hope.
Eventually, you give up. Turn to **173**.

90

The light of the fire draws you closer, like a
moth. You edge forward, trying to stay out
of sight of the shadowy figures that you can
see moving around the flames. From this
distance, it is impossible to work out who or
what they are. Before you reach them, the
path forks away.

To follow the fork, turn to **40**.

To continue towards the fire, turn to **208**.

91

Stepping onto the beach, you feel the welcome breeze from the ocean, a nice contrast to the damp air between the trees. To your left, you can see the dock where you arrived yesterday. On your right, there appears to be another jetty, which ends in a square, covered gazebo.

To head to the dock, turn to **184**.

To head to the gazebo, turn to **3**.

92

The door is locked and seems to offer no way to break past it. You can continue to explore the building for other ways in, or you can return to the path.

To circle the building, turn to **215**.

To head back to the path, turn to **202**.

93

"I'm done!" Fern cries, dropping the baseball bat and recoiling onto the benches. "Leave me alone."

You try to talk to her, but she turns her

head and begins to tend to her wounds.
There's nothing else to be done here, so
you leave the building, heading straight out
of the front door and back onto the path.
Turn to **202**.

94

Sun loungers and white plastic chairs are
scattered across the poolside area. Clearly,
whoever was sitting around the pool left
in a hurry. Abandoned cocktails adorn the
few tables that are still standing, the rest
are littered across the stones as nothing
more than broken shards of glass. One
sun lounger appears to still be occupied,
although the occupant isn't moving. The
lounger is positioned in full sun by the edge
of the pool. A narrow path, unmarked other
than by a rough stone shingle, heads away
from the pool into the densely packed trees
that border it.

To step closer to the body in the chair, turn
to **73**.

To head away from the pool and along the
path, turn to **138**.

95

You slip into a rhythm of reaching out to drag yourself forward, allowing the simple monotony to take over. You are so lost in your reverie that you don't notice the metal beneath your belly sagging until it eventually gives way, and you plummet into a dark room. Remove **1 HEALTH POINT.** You stagger to your feet and are immediately set upon by a pack of startled rats who see you as an easy meal. They may be small and weak, but their numbers and element of surprise give them the advantage. You suffer a -1 **STRENGTH** penalty for this fight. Fight the **RATS** as a single enemy.

RATS:

Strength: 8
Health: 14

When you have defeated them, turn to **53**.

96

Just beyond the edge of the path, you notice a movement amongst the trees. It doesn't seem as though it is moving towards you, but something is definitely twitching in the shadows. You edge closer,

trying your hardest not to make a sound. Holding your breath, you push aside a broad palm leaf and stop in your tracks. Up ahead, a young man dressed in a sharp shirt and tailored shorts is bent over. He seems to be leaning over another man who is lying on the floor.

You step forward, feeling the resistance of a dry stick underfoot too late. The sound of the crack rattles through the forest, alerting the man to your presence. He snaps his head around, and you see the terror that he has become. His face is pale green and blistered, his eyes wide and bloodshot. Patches of skin are hanging from his cheekbones, and his teeth are sharp and covered in the same blood that is smeared around his mouth.

He is clearly possessed or diseased, and the look in his eyes is a mixture of fear and rage. He tries to scramble to his feet to lunge at you, but his feet slip, giving you a split second to make a choice.

To stand your ground, turn to **108**.

To turn and run through the thick undergrowth, turn to **205**.

97

The air inside the hut is still and humid, permeated with the scent of lavender from a stout candle that has burnt low. You snuff it out just as you hear the sound of something following you through the door. When you turn, you are face-to-face with a pack of zombies.

Roll for a **RANDOM ZOMBIE ENCOUNTER.**

Once the fight is over, you realise that there is nothing else of interest in the room. You leave and return to the path. Turn to **81**.

98

The high tide has restricted the beach to a few yards wide, and you are forced to wade through the shallow water. In the distance, perhaps a hundred yards out to sea, you can make out the broken hull of a wooden ship. You have no idea if it beached on the island a century ago or if it was placed there for tourists to visit, but it is clearly important enough for the tourism board to signpost. You head across the beach for a closer look.

On this side of the island, the waves crash into the beach with more energy, soaking your legs to your knees. It's hard to work out what you can see underwater, but occasional flitting shadows promise fish. Thinking that they might be useful for food, you stand still and lean closer.

Explosive energy rips through the waves, knocking you back into the shallow water. You turn and push back against the primal beast on top of you. It lashes out, powerful muscles flexing and its wide maw opening. You take in the image of a saltwater crocodile, a dozen feet long and built to kill. There is something different about this beast, though. When it opens its mouth, an eerie green glow floods out, bathing you in a radioactive shadow. Instinctively, you make the link between the mutated monster and the virus unleashed on the island, but you struggle to understand why it appears to be radioactive rather than undead.

You don't have time to ponder, though, as the beast is circling back for the kill.

IRRADIATED SALTWATER CROCODILE:
Strength: 16
Health: 16

If you manage to slay the monster, you drag yourself back onto the beach and continue your journey. Turn to **20**.

99

The sound of the waves lapping against the beach grows louder as you progress along the path. It curves gently away from the main resort, looping behind a sizeable wooden hut. Opposite, you spot a stout gate that seems to lead to another path, this one heading away from the beach.
To look more closely at the gate, turn to **132**. To ignore it and follow the path round towards the beach, turn to **105**.

100

When you have calmed down, you relay what happened as best you can, but your story is lacking in detail. Without more information, the people on board are reluctant to abandon their party. Instead, you settle back and let the music and good

atmosphere wash over you, desperate
to return home and forget about the
nightmare you have endured.

The unsatisfactory ending to your ordeal
doesn't sit well, but you comfort yourself
with the knowledge that at least you are
alive. Many of the others on the island are
not. Perhaps any other survivors will do a
better job of uncovering what happened to
you all. Without that information, there is
no telling how far the virus will spread and
what the damage will be on the mainland.

101

You pluck one of the mushrooms from the
ground, admiring the beauty of the crystals
lodged in its flesh. As you tear it from its
roots, you hear it let out a muffled cry as if
in pain.

You try to shake the feeling of guilt, but it
doesn't pass. You ram it into your **PACK** and
turn to leave, only to find your way blocked
by a ring of similar mushrooms. They have
sprouted from nowhere, seeming to grow
out of the rock itself.

Before you can react, they start to slowly

grow until they are a few feet tall, the jagged crystals suddenly ominous rather than beautiful.

Roll a die to work out how many **CRYSTAL 'SHROOMS** you must defeat before you can continue.

CRYSTAL 'SHROOM:

Strength: 9
Health: 12

Special: Each successful attack by the **CRYSTAL 'SHROOMS** temporarily blinds you with the light from their crystals. For the following attack, you suffer a -1 **STRENGTH** penalty.

If you defeat the mushrooms, you flee back to the path and continue into the caves. Turn to **143**.

102

This close to the water, mosquitoes buzz around you, trying desperately to make a home in your orifices. You swat them away as best you can but eventually relinquish hope and let them feed. At the bottom of the steps, the pathway leads down towards the small swimming pool or away into the trees.

To head to the swimming pool, turn to **232**.

To turn away and head into the trees, turn to **23**.

103

The strange zombies are still dancing around the fire, trying to devour their strange meal cooking over the flames. You try to ignore the smell and work out your next move. There is a path sneaking away behind the zombies, but to travel that way, you will need to sneak past them. To try, turn to **212**. Alternatively, the road ahead splits in two. The first path is directly ahead and leads past the business centre. To follow it, turn to **40**. A few yards past that track is another, which seems to head past the tourist centre. To follow that path, turn to **65**.

104

There appear to be lights on in the next hut, but you can't be sure whether you can see movement. To enter, turn to **198**. To walk past, turn to **110**.

Following the path round to the beach, you notice the heat of the sun increases. There is no shelter here, and you are fully exposed to the nearly-midday rays. You are almost relieved to see an open door just off the beach. The large shed might offer some respite from the sun if you choose to use it.

Ahead, you spot a wooden walkway leading out to a gazebo a few hundred yards out into the ocean. It looks like it has been decorated for a wedding, and you can just about make out the silhouettes of two people moving in the shade of the roof.

Further along the beach, you can just make out the pier leading to the dock where you arrived yesterday.

To step into the shed, turn to **166**.

To push on towards the gazebo, turn to **204**.

To head past the gazebo and continue along the beach towards the dock, turn to **184**.

106

You stare at the woman for a moment before giving her the smallest nod. She leaps to her feet, and you recoil, expecting an attack. Instead, she throws her arms around you and embraces you awkwardly. When she disentangles herself, she looks sheepish. "Sorry," she murmurs. "Here, take this." She offers you a bottle of water, warm but clean. You drink it quickly, savouring the relief. Restore **4 HEALTH POINTS.**

To sit a while and talk to the girl, turn to **67**.

To head back out to the beach, turn to **149**.

107

The captain looks at you deeply, a pale mask of sorrow etched in the lines of her face. She shakes her head slowly and pulls back the board. "I'm sorry," she says quietly. "I can't take the risk."

You cry out, begging her for mercy, to take you back to the mainland where you can be cured. She isn't listening or is making a good attempt at not caring. "There is nothing I can offer you now," she finishes, her words lost in the noise of the engine roaring to life. Before you can say anything, the boat slowly begins to turn out of the dock. Desperation takes over, and you sprint forward, feeling the wooden boards disappear beneath your feet as you launch yourself towards the stern of the ship. Your fingertips graze the edge, and you cling on, your feet dangling in the ocean.

Wide-eyed terror has replaced the look of pity in the captain's eyes when she stares down at you. Without wasting a second, she reaches for something under the benches. Her hand returns, holding a spear gun, the type she might use to spear fish in the open ocean. She points it towards you, but your own terror has taken control of your fingers, and they won't let go.

By the time she fires and the spear pierces your body, sending you tumbling into the water, fear has such a grip on you that you feel nothing. Her final act may have been one of mercy after all.

108

You square your shoulders and get ready for the inevitable attack. Before you can ready your weapon, the man is upon you, pushing you to the ground and trying to claw at your face. You reach out and snatch up a stout branch. Thrusting it in front of you, you hear the satisfying crunch of it pushing through the man's chest. His eyes widen, and he lets out a guttural scream, smothering you in the foul stench of his breath. You watch the life drain from his eyes, and a pale waxen sheen wash over his skin. He slides from your body and lies dead in the undergrowth. Whatever strange malady had overcome him seems to have deserted his body, and you are just glad to be alive.

You turn around and push your way back to the path. Turn to **123**.

109

If you haven't investigated the shed yet and would like to, turn to **220**.

Otherwise, turn to **162**.

You push past the overhanging palm leaves and fern fronds that line the path, all the while battling against the humidity that clings to your skin. The rustling of the leaves overhead creates an unsettling backdrop to the tropical paradise that the holiday-makers usually envisage. Suddenly, you freeze, the sight of something ahead bringing you to a halt.

There's a figure crouched on a low branch, larger than a dog but smaller than a human. You edge closer until you make out the form of a monkey, but there's something terribly wrong. Its fur is matted and sparse, hanging off its skeletal frame in clumps. Where bare skin is exposed, it is raw and stretched across bones that poke through in gruesome blisters.

Its head jerks up, fixating on your movement. You see its eyes, cloudy and dead yet glowing with a pale hatred. It draws its lips back in a snarl, revealing blood-stained teeth and a tongue coated with boils. Its laboured, wheezing breath wafts the stench of rot towards you, infiltrating your nose and coating your mouth. Its fingers grip the branch with unnatural strength, its bone-tipped digits capped with blackened nails.

You catch its glare and panic. It's sizing you up, far more intelligent than anything else you have faced on the island. You ready yourself for the attack.

ZOMBIFIED MONKEY:

Strength: 12
Health: 20

Once you have defeated the grotesque parody of your own ancestors, you are able to continue along the path. Turn to **26**.

111

The door swings open easily, revealing a cramped hut filled with mess. The floor is covered in wooden crates filled with wetsuits and fins, whilst the walls are hung with oxygen tanks, spear guns and other diving paraphernalia. One box contains sets of smaller oxygen tanks that can be carried easily and used with a snorkel mask. You may take one if you wish, although they are

bulky items. SCUBA EQUIPMENT takes up two weapon slots to carry.

SCUBA EQUIPMENT:

Special: Allows you to breathe underwater for a short period of time.

You may also take a **SPEAR GUN** and a **TORCH** if you wish.

SPEAR GUN:

Strength: +1
Durability: Unlimited
Special: May only be used underwater

Once you are happy that you have everything you need, you return to the crossroads. Turn to **226**.

112

The entrance to the business centre is dark, the overhanging upper storey casting everything into shadow. The automatic sliding doors have been propped open by a chair, but there is no sign of anybody about. You enter the building, taking care to check that there is nothing immediately dangerous inside.

Past the doors, the main reception area is a large open space. The walls are adorned with various advertising boards, and several large televisions endlessly display silent promotional films in a loop. There are signs of last night's chaos everywhere.

A scattered array of chairs, coats and suitcases litters the floor. Several items appear to have been thrown at the large glass windows, cracking the glass. At the far end of the room, another pair of doors are closed.

A flashback races across your mind of people screaming and kicking their way through those doors. You remember that the main auditorium is beyond them, but most of your recollections are still clouded by white mist.

Just before the double doors, there is another single door. You glance through the glass panel and see that it opens onto a stairwell leading up to the first floor.

To head through the doors, turn to **29**.

To head up the stairs, turn to **175**.

113

You turn and retreat, trying to quiet the noise of your blood rushing through your ears. It's altogether too dark and creepy down here, and your only desire is to return to the surface. Eventually, you reach the foot of the stairs and race up them, gratefully emerging back into the white marble of the reception area. Turn to **195**.

114

"I don't trust you," Fern cries. She grabs a mug from the coffee table and throws it at your head. You duck out of the way, but when you look back, she's heading out of the door and disappearing along the path. You could try to chase her, but it is unlikely that you will catch her. Instead, you head back out to the path. Turn to **202**.

115

In a final fit of rage, the old man throws his broken body towards you. It crumples against your body, falling to a heap of bones and flesh. His femur, stained yellow but strong and covered with sharp splinters, rolls away from the rest of his body. If you can stomach holding onto the wretched item, you may add it to your weapons.

FEMUR:

Strength: +2
Durability: Unlimited

Once you are finished in the room, turn to **117**.

116

Ahead of you, the path leads south past a series of stark buildings. They are all small and unmarked, clearly intended for staff only. Sure enough, you stop outside one marked as a staff breakroom. There are several wooden benches and trash cans out front, all of them overflowing. A set of sliding doors leads into the building, which appears to be dark.

To try to enter the building, turn to **92**.

To ignore it and continue along the path, turn to **202**.

117

If you haven't checked out the hut yet, you can do so by turning to **16**.

If you haven't investigated the medical centre, you can do so by turning to **218**.

If you have been to both buildings or you wish to leave, you can return to the main track by turning to **137**.

118

It is pitch black in the tunnel here, and you struggle to work out your direction. For all you know, you might be passing side tunnels that lead to freedom, but there is no way to tell. Instead, your only option is to press on, carefully edging forward. After a seemingly endless amount of time, you find yourself slipping into a peaceful rhythm of reaching ahead of yourself and pulling your body along. Even against the now roaring sound of whatever is buzzing, you find a sort of peace in the process.

Until you reach the source of the noise.

Just as the noise reaches its ultimate crescendo, you reach out one final time and scream out in agony. You realise too late that the sound it coming from an enormous fan, drawing air through the building by the way of rapidly spinning blades - blades into which you have just thrust both of your hands.

You scream in agony, rolling around in the tunnel until everything begins to slowly drift away. It is unlikely that anybody will find your body, and your final thoughts are of this metal tube becoming your tomb for all eternity. At least it is better than the zombies, you reflect.

119

You reach the end of the dock in time to see the party boat heading back out to sea. You curse your luck and hurl abuse at the retreating boat until your voice is hoarse. After a few moments, you regain your composure and realise that all is not lost. There may still be a way off the island.

If you have a **KEY CARD,** turn to **21**.

It not, turn to **61**.

120

You emerge from the cavern, blinking in the bright sunlight. Down in the cool darkness, you had forgotten about the gnawing heat of the full sun. It burns your skin and sucks the moisture from your mouth. Cursing yourself for not bringing any water, you take the path that stretches away in front of you. It curves gently to the left past a series of thatched, wooden huts that look decked out for holiday-makers. Each one has a veranda out front with a hot tub and swing chair. They all look like they have been evacuated in a hurry. Only three of them appear to be open. The first is set back from the main path along a barked track. To head over to it, turn to **77**.

Otherwise, you can continue onwards towards the other huts. Turn to **104**.

121

You play with the dials for as long as you dare but with no luck. You listen out for the smallest hint of somebody on the other end, but all you hear is white noise and the noise of strange things moving around in the shadows behind you. Eventually, it all becomes too much, and you decide to abandon the task and head back to the reception. Turn to **113**.

122

The sailor's chest is unlocked, but the hinges have seized. You take a small pocket knife from your backpack and use it to prise the lid open. The blade bends in the process, so you toss it onto your bed to fix later. Inside the chest, you find a small hatchet. It is nicely weighted, and the blade is sharp to the touch. You add it to your **WEAPONS**.

HATCHET:
Strength: +1
Durability: 10

If you would like to head into the living quarters, turn to **224**.

If you would rather open the glass doors, turn to **39**.

The dirt track continues in a winding fashion for a while, slowly taking you down towards the sandy cove that you saw from the balcony. It seems to meander in an annoying fashion, sometimes almost doubling back on itself, but eventually, you push through a damp cluster of monstera leaves. Out from the cover of the trees, the early-morning sun beats down on your head, escalating your headache even further. Black dots pinwheel across your vision until they slowly merge together to form a group of about half a dozen people, all dressed in tattered and torn beach clothes.

Stumbling onto the sand, you recoil from their angry shouts. You stand still until the dizziness passes and your focus returns. When you open your eyes again, you take in the scene on the beach.

Halfway between yourself and the ocean, the people appear to have constructed a barricade made from sun parasols, deck chairs, surfboards and whatever other debris they could find on the beach. Rather than blocking access to the water, they have built it as a large ring.

As you approach, they all sprint away, disappearing through a small hatch in the front of the pile. One of the group, a middle-aged woman dressed in a kimono, seems to be in charge. She climbs to the top of something inside the ring of debris so that her head and upper body are visible.

"Bugger of!" she shouts in a broad Australian accent. "We're full."

You take a moment to consider what she has said, but no matter how hard you try, you can't make it make sense. The words are all there, but when you put them together, you are as confused as ever.

"What do you mean?" you shout back. You take a few steps forward. Somebody hidden inside the barricade fires a gun, the bullet erupting a volcano of sand a few yards in front of you.

"Stay back!" she screams again. "We mean it. Next time, we won't miss."

"What's going on?" You raise your hands above your head and slowly take a few steps back to show good faith.

"They're out there hunting us," she explains, still in her shrill screech. "You must have seen them. Something happened last night that turned everyone into one of those..." she pauses for a second before continuing, "zombies."

Another piece of your memory puzzle drops into place. You remember the man standing at the podium, talking about how you were all going to be his greatest experiment yet. There is a hazy memory of him raising a remote and pressing a button, then nothing but the same pale fog.

"I can't remember what happened," you mutter. "It's just a fog."

"That's what the other survivors said," another voice adds. A man stands up next to the woman, holding a rifle uneasily. "Just a pale fog, and then they woke up with a blinding headache. How do you think we feel? We came here for a holiday, not to be attacked by a bunch of undead sales executives."

Something that he said occurs to you. "You said the other survivors? There are more out there?"

The man nods. "We saw a few when we went back up to the tourism centre this morning. We wanted to complain."

"What happened?"

"Somebody tried to attack me!" he cries, incredulous at the thought.

If you have already encountered one of the zombies, turn to **84**.

If not, turn to **152**.

124

You follow the path as it traces the edge of the pool, carefully stepping down from the wooden deck onto a hard stone path.

The whole area is lined with large boulders, ornately balanced and packed with ferns stuffed into every crevice. When you reach a crossroads, the stones block your view in all directions.

Ahead, you can just make out a narrow pathway through lush vegetation. To your left, the path seems to head south towards the back of the tourism centre.

To your right, the path ends abruptly at a

small hut that seems to be a watersports hub.

To continue onwards, turn to **48**.

To turn left towards the tourism centre, turn to **36**.

To head towards the watersports hub, turn to **78**.

125

Indeed, the hut appears to be a watersports rental unit. The door swings open easily, revealing a cramped hut filled with equipment.

Wooden crates, filled with wetsuits and fins, crowd the floor whilst the walls are hung with other diving paraphernalia, including a spear gun. One of the boxes contains a set of smaller oxygen tanks that can be carried easily and used with a snorkel mask.

You may take one if you wish, although they are bulky items. **SCUBA EQUIPMENT** takes up two weapon slots to carry.

SCUBA EQUIPMENT:

Special: Allows you to breathe underwater for a short period of time.

You may also take a **SPEAR GUN** and a **TORCH** if you wish.

SPEAR GUN:

Strength: +1
Durability: Unlimited
Special: May only be used underwater

Once you are happy that you have everything you need, you return to the path and continue onwards. Turn to **187**.

126

The front of the bar is narrow, just enough for somebody to serve drinks and hand over food.

Through the door into the kitchen, you can hear a soft sound. It could be somebody humming or perhaps the soft groan of somebody close to death.

You edge closer, sneaking a peak around the doorframe.

Beyond, in a kitchen thick with grease,

somebody is busying themselves behind a hot stove.

To call out, turn to **174**.

To enter the room quietly, turn to **18**.

To leave the bar, turn to **109**.

127

You fight back the urge to vomit as you approach the victim. You try not to look at their face or the multiple wounds, instead focusing on their pockets. The only thing you find is a small scrap of paper with the number 37 scribbled on it. You make a note and step away from the body.

To check out the rest of the room, turn to **5**. Otherwise, you can leave the building by turning to **14**.

128

Her first blow crashes into your arm, dealing out **1 HEALTH POINT** damage, but you manage to roll out of the way and duck behind the benches. "Listen to me," you cry, "I'm not one of them. I'm just trying to get off the island."

"Prove it," she shouts, swinging the bat over her head. "Drop your weapon."

To do as she says, remove one of your weapons and turn to **211**.

To refuse, turn to **228**.

129

You push on, trying all of the doors to see if they open. None of them do. On a few occasions, you hear the sound of movement behind them, but you can't work out whether they are survivors hiding away or worse. At the end of the corridor, you look through the window out at the ocean beyond. In the distance, you can just make out the outline of a ship slipping across the horizon, oblivious to the dangers you are facing. It's heartbreaking to think about how close they are and yet so out of reach.

Turning around, your arm brushes against a fire extinguisher strapped to the wall. A loud scraping noise against the door next to you startles you, and you grip the red canister. You may add it to your **WEAPONS** if you choose.

FIRE EXTINGUISHER:

Strength: +4

Durability: 8

Special: At any point in a fight, you may choose to pull the pin and unleash the foam inside the extinguisher. If you do, don't roll any dice to attack that turn. Instead, you deal out an automatic 10 HEALTH POINTS damage, but it destroys the extinguisher, and it must be removed from your WEAPONS.

You head back along the corridor and down the steps. Turn to **182**.

130

The man on the other end seems sceptical. "You honestly expect me to believe that zombies have taken over the island? Do you have proof?"

How do you respond?

"Come and see for yourself. The island is crawling with proof." Turn to **47**.

"I'm alone on a boat off the coast at the moment, but trust me, they are there. It's a small chunk of hell." Turn to **170**.

131

Your endless movement in the water hasn't gone unnoticed, and you soon begin to feel the tentative bumps that indicate unwelcome company in the water. You stop moving, slowly treading water in the vain hope that they will leave you alone, but they've sensed your desperation and the promise of an easy lunch. One by one, the sharks move in, attacking you until the dark water is stained red with your blood. You don't feel a thing.

132

There is a sign on the gate that reads:

"Access to holiday rentals and caves. Permit holders only."

You rattle the gate, but the lock is secure, and there seems to be no other way through. You return to the path. Turn to **105**.

133

You draw the SPEAR GUN from your weapons and try to steady yourself in the water. The zombie shark is much more agile than you and attacks with speed. For each

round of the battle, test your **STRENGTH.** If
you pass, you are able to turn in the water
and attack as normal.

If you fail, the shark manages to attack
from your rear, automatically dealing
2 HEALTH POINTS damage.

ZOMBIE SHARK:

Strength: 15
Health: 18

If you manage to defeat the shark, you have just enough oxygen left to swim to the side of the boat and reach the ladder. Turn to **144**.

134

You enter the cave system, and immediately, the ground drops away from you. You regain your footing and grasp the walls to support you. If you have a **TORCH** in your **PACK,** turn to **12**. Otherwise, turn to **192**.

135

The path is well-marked, but the trees and climbing plants that line it have started to reclaim the space for their own. It narrows until you are walking sideways between damp branches and trying to avoid thick webs strung across your way. Just as you are about to give up and turn back, you hear the groaning sound again, only now it is much closer. It sounds like it is coming from just inside the trees to your right.

To head off the path and investigate the sound, turn to **96**.

To continue straight ahead, turn to **123**.

You scramble over the twitching bodies of the dead zombies just as the Azure Queen begins to turn into the dock. You can see the distressed face of the captain, her red hair blowing in the breeze, and her eyes twisted with horror at what she has just seen. Nevertheless, she is bringing the boat in, ready for you to embark. Before you have the chance, you hear a loud roar behind you and turn to see a muscle-bound brute barrelling towards you. An image of last night flashes behind your eyes, and you make the connection; he was the man behind the virus, the man who started all of this. Judging by his swollen eyes and ragged flesh, he wasn't able to escape his own creation.

You try to react, to urge the boat closer, but there's no time. The man is upon you, and you realise with a sickening horror that you have one final battle before you will be able to board the boat.

MUSCLE-BOUND BRUTE:
Strength: 15
Health: 24

If you overcome the man, turn to **45**.

137

Ahead of you, a small fire is burning in an old oil drum. If you came this way before, turn to **103**. Otherwise, turn to **221**.

138

The pathway is narrow and dark, but you pass through easily enough. On the other side, you emerge on a wide stone path. In one direction, the towering glass bulk of the tourism centre rises above the palm trees. In the opposite direction, the path winds away towards the beach.

To head towards the tourism centre, turn to **169**.

To head towards the beach, turn to **99**.

139

You scream until you are hoarse, but the people on the boat remain indifferent to your plight. You try throwing stones out into the ocean in vain, but they are too far away to see anything. Despondent, you return to the path and head back towards the burning barrel. At the fire, the path turns away in two directions. To head along the first track, turn to **40**. To head along the second track, a few yards ahead, turn to **65**.

140

You flee the buzzing horde, rubbing your skin where their electric sparks strike. Desperate to get out of the sun, you pick up the pace and start to jog towards the jetty. Once there, you climb a small set of steps onto the wooden boardwalk and take a moment in the shade of a cluster of palm trees to recover. The heady scent of the towering red flowers starts to make you feel sick, so you don't linger for long. When you are feeling strong enough, you turn towards the end of the jetty. Turn to **186**.

141

You climb a seemingly endless set of rough stone steps until you reach the mouth of a dark tunnel. You turn on your torch, but the light seems to get sucked away and lost, reflecting nothingness.

To carry on regardless, turn to **7**.

Otherwise, you return to the fork in the road. To explore the "room", turn to **213**. To explore the rock wall, turn to **146**.

Somehow, the pool water feels thicker than normal, requiring more effort to push through. You notice it has a strange green hue and a thick layer of scum floating on the surface. As you wade deeper, it begins to wrap itself around your body until you are entirely encased in a syrupy, gelatinous goo.

You wrestle against it in a desperate bid to free yourself from its embrace, but it just seems to cling tighter until you are gasping for each breath that never fully forms.

Within minutes, your energy and strength are sapped, and you are powerless to resist the ebb and flow of the water carrying you further towards the deeper end, where you gradually sink to the bottom, your silent cries for salvation nothing more than small bubbles on the surface.

Your death isn't quick, but you may take some solace in the fact that your body will provide nutrients for the pool slime for many months to come.

143

After a while, you notice the ground to your left falling away until the path borders a cliff, dropping down into a still lake far below. You continue along the edge of the precipice until you reach a rope bridge that crosses the water. The path you are on continues ahead and seems to rise upwards as it does.

To cross the bridge, turn to **206**.

To carry on ahead, turn to **68**.

144

You scramble over the balustrade on the edge of the boat and bask in the heat of the sun on your skin. Almost immediately, you begin to dry out. You check the gauge on the tank and are dismayed to find that it is almost empty. Taking in the boat, you realise that most of it has collapsed into the ocean. There is the square section that you are standing on, which appears to be the stern, and the pointy bit, which you have heard referred to as the bow. Between the two ends, there isn't much other than a dark void. You sidle to the edge of the

stern and gaze down. The ocean is a dark, 
swirling mix of strange shadows and flitting
light. More importantly, there appears to be
no way back up if you fall in.

The ship appears to have had two masts
when it was whole, and one of them
has fallen in such a way as to create a
precarious bridge between the two halves.
On the far side, you can see evidence that
people have perhaps been here recently.
There are a couple of old wooden crates,
but there also appears to be a more modern
metal box. Around you, the rest of the
stern appears to be empty, but you may
investigate in more detail if you choose.

To attempt walking over to what is probably
the bow of the ship, turn to **24**.

To investigate the stern further, turn to **63**.

To try to swim back to shore, turn to **214**.

145

The track snakes through well-manicured
beds of palm trees until it veers sharply to
the right. Before the bend, there is another
hut. The door is open, and the lights are on,

but you can't hear any sound inside. To look inside the hut, turn to **16**. Next to the hut is a larger building. The sign on the front says that it is a medical centre. The door is shut, but there are lights on inside. To investigate the medical centre, turn to **218**.

146

As you thought, the rock face is covered in hand-holds and ledges. You slowly start to climb upwards and are soon pulling yourself over the top of the ridge and onto a soft path.

Ahead of you, shafts of sunlight announce your arrival back at the surface. You hurry towards them and the island. Turn to **120**.

147

Cursing yourself for the fact that you took the scuba gear but not the spear gun, you try to swim back towards the ladder on the side of the boat. It doesn't matter how furiously you thrash, your speed is nothing compared to the zombie shark.

You are barely halfway to the ladder when the first bite tears into your flesh. You feel

the agonising stings across your legs, and then nothing but white bliss.

Suddenly, you are pain-free. You stop swimming as a sense of final acceptance washes over you.

With your final act, you close your eyes and brace yourself for the humourless grin approaching in the shadow of the boat.

148

You push the small rowing boat up onto the balustrade and tip it into the ocean below. It lands upside down but stays afloat. You throw both oars after it and dive clear of the hull, ignoring the ringing in your ears as you sink beneath the surface.

When you rise, you quickly grab the oars before they can float away and right the rowboat. Using the ladder on the hull of the larger boat, you manage to scramble in and start to row slowly back to shore.

The heat beats down on your back, burning your skin and drying your mouth. You decide not to push yourself too hard, reasoning that it's better to get back to shore alive than die out here.

Eventually, you are close enough to leap overboard and stand in the shallow surf. You wade back to the beach, dragging the boat with you before stowing it on the rocks. Once your skin has dried, you retrieve your clothes and get dressed. You head back along the beach towards the caves.

Turn to **223**.

149

You leave the shed and head out into the burning heat of the sun. Add **EMILIA** to your **ALLIES**.

EMILIA:

Strength: 9
Health: 20
Immunity: 6
Occupation: Student of Philosophy

Almost immediately, you regret drinking all of the water at once, but there is no more to be found. To head towards the gazebo, turn to **204**. To continue past and head towards the dock, turn to **184**.

150

"Can you get this to work?" you ask Elrond, noticing a broad smile appear on his face.

"It's what I was born to do," he replies, settling into the cracked leather seat and rubbing his neck. "Ten years as a radio engineer, and I never thought I'd use my skills to save the world."

It doesn't take him long to discover an open channel, and he quickly tunes the radio until he is satisfied. Turn to **37**.

151

The path continues in a gentle curve, separated from the crashing waves only by densely planted beds and the occasional hut. As you meander along it, something heavy crashes out of the undergrowth behind you.

You don't wait to find out what it is, so you take flight immediately. You sprint, lungs burning and ankles crying out for you to stop, until you stop outside of a block of a building that you recognise from last night.

You turn back, but whatever startled you hasn't followed. The building is the business centre, the scene of last night's carnage. Your memory is still nothing more than a blur, but inside the building might offer more answers.

Ahead, a staff gate blocks your way, meaning your only other option is to head back along the track that you just sprinted up.

To enter the building, turn to **112**.

To return to the track, turn to **116**.

152

You try to engage the couple in a conversation about what is on the island, but they seem reluctant to trust you. "Listen, we need to help each other," you plead, but they just stare back at you angrily.

Annoyed by their refusal to talk and with the heat of the sun, your temper starts to fray.

It is only a few dozen metres to the

barricade, and the man doesn't seem alert with his rifle. You can try to rush them and force your way in by turning to **181**.

To back away and leave them in peace, turn to **209**.

153

The final zombie drops to the floor, knocking over a bedside table in the process. A pair of battery-powered hair straighteners roll across the floor and come to rest against your feet. You may add them to your **WEAPONS** if you choose.

BATTERY-POWERED HAIR STRAIGHTENERS:
Strength: +1
Durability: 10
Special: The heated paddles elicit a smell of lightly burnt flesh whenever you apply them to a zombie's skin. Enjoy!

You return to the main path outside the hut. Turn to **104**.

154

As you approach the chef, you realise that he is frying food long past its best.

Everything he is preparing is rotten and stinks, and he is no different. He has one good eye, his left; the other is nothing but an empty socket. His tall chef's hat is mouldy and covered in dark spots, his apron no better.

Then, he turns and faces you, holding a silver platter in one hand. You struggle to keep hold of your stomach. Facing you is the eyeless head of a young man, decapitated and served on a bed of rotting vegetables. As you watch, the undead chef forces a maggoty apple into the man's mouth.

The unholy scene in front of you is enough to drive you to madness, and you attack before the zombie can ready itself. If you are successful on your first attack, you deal double the damage.

ZOMBIE CHEF:

Strength: 9
Health: 10

If you defeat the abomination, you flee back to the serving area of the bar. Turn to **44**.

155

You reach the end of the jetty in time to see the Azure Queen round the headland. The captain has clearly been keeping a watch on the dock, and your frantic waving has caught her attention. Unfortunately, the boat is still a short distance from the shore, and it looks like it will take a minute or so to arrive. Until then, you will have to hold your ground at the end of the boardwalk. The desperate horde of zombies is already halfway towards you, and only their own in-fighting is slowing them down.

Every second counts and your eyes are on a pivot between the approaching options; survival or death. Unfortunately, it looks like the zombies are going to arrive first, so you will need to fight off a few before you can escape to safety.

The zombies approach in the following order and must be defeated before moving on to the next. Use the **RANDOM ZOMBIE ENCOUNTER** table for their stats.

Two **HALF-TURNED ZOMBIES**
One **OUTRIGHT TERROR**
An **ABHORRENT GHOUL**

Once you have defeated them, turn to **136**.

156

"Forget this," you mumble, drawing your weapon and facing the angry sales executive. You wait for her to attack.

ANGRY SALES EXECUTIVE:

Strength: 15
Health: 18
If you reduce her health to less than 3, turn to **93**.

157

You aren't watching where you are going, and you stumble into a trolley, sending it clattering across the kitchen. The chef looks up but says nothing. He's clearly spotted you, and to leave now would be awkward, so you head towards him. Turn to **154**.

158

Stepping over the twitching remains of your foe, you follow the track to its end on a high outlook. Somebody has thoughtfully provided a set of mechanical binoculars, although it requires several coins that you don't have. Even without them, you can make out the shape of a boat in the middle distance. You can hear the soft drones of party music, punctuated by the piercing cry of laughter. It's a party boat and might represent your only way off the island.

They are too far away to reach simply by shouting, but a **FLAREGUN** would attract their attention. If you have one in your **PACK** turn to **49**. If not, turn to **139**.

159

It rapidly becomes clear that there is nothing up here but heat. You head back towards the elevator and step inside, relishing the cool air as the air conditioning kicks in. Just as you push the button to start your descent, something heavy crashes through the ceiling, landing on the floor heavily but quickly rising to its feet.

The elevator kicks in, trapping you in a small room with a raging zombie. Judging by his uniform, he was once one of the bell-boys working in the resort. Now, he's nothing more than a furious weapon hell-bent on your demise.

ZOMBIE BELL-BOY:

Strength: 12

Health: 13

If you manage to defeat him, turn to **42**.

160

"Your guess is as good as mine," you mutter, trying not to watch him eat.

"There was a big commotion last night," he offers. "I woke up about midnight, and there was a lot of banging and shouting outside. You weren't back at that point," he finished with an accusatory tone.

"At least I made it to the conference," you argue.

Elrond shrugs. "What did I miss?"

You shrug back. "I can't really remember. It's a bit of a blur."

"It certainly sounded like there was a lot of trouble kicking off. I don't really fancy heading out there alone today." You notice the hopeful notes in his voice. "I've got a weapon," he adds, pulling a curved sword out from behind the cushions on the sofa. "I picked it up in the gift shop yesterday," he finishes, noticing the look of horror in your eyes. "I was a radio engineer in the army."

You look him over, from his orange fingers to the desperately hopeful look on his face.

To offer to take him with you, turn to **172**.

To reject his proposal, turn to **27**.

161

Here, at last, there is some relief from the burning sun. The towering bulk of the business centre casts the narrow pathway into deep shadows. On your left, a smaller hut is marked as a medical centre, but the door must be on the other side. There is no way in from here. You press on, ignoring the calls of the monkeys overhead and the parrots in the sky, until one cry grabs your full attention. You stop dead, your eyes locked onto the monstrosity in front of you.

A few yards ahead, perched atop a squat mango tree, is what must once have been a parrot. Now, its eye sockets are nothing more than empty voids, its beak a broken and twisted mess of splintered shell and oozing flesh. Its feathers, once a vibrant

red and
blue, are
matted
and blood-
soaked
where
they remain
and plucked
pale flesh
where they don't.
Whatever virus
is raging
through the
humans on the island
has clearly spread to
the local fauna.

Before you can back away, the
parrot screams and flaps its broken wings.
It manages to get airborne just enough
to fly into your face, clawing at you with
savage talons.

ZOMBIE PARROT:

Strength: 8
Health: 8

If you manage to put the poor bird out of its
misery, turn to **51**.

162

You turn back towards the path, but before you can reach it, the surface of the pool parts and a thick, pulsing serpent emerges. The anaconda doesn't appear to have been infected, but it is larger than any snake you have ever seen before and doesn't seem pleased to see you. It slithers from the water and blocks your escape.

ANACONDA:

Strength: 7
Health: 10
Note: This animal is not **INFECTED**.

Once you have defeated the reptile, you return to the path. Turn to **71**.

163

You follow the edge of the beach until you are surrounded by dense palms and high-canopied trees.

After a short while, you reach a waterfall, perhaps a dozen feet tall, that empties into a small pool. That, too, eventually flows out to the ocean a few yards away.

Behind the waterfall, you find an entrance to a cave system. It is tall enough for you to walk into, but it is almost entirely dark.

To head inside, turn to **134**.

To turn back towards the beach, turn to **98**.

164

You continue deeper into the building, stepping slowly until your eyes adjust fully, and you realise that you are in an old kitchen. It's the kind you'd see at the back of an all-night diner on an American highway, perhaps once full of noise and bustle but now dead and subdued.

Off to one side, a flickering blue light draws your attention. You walk over, pushing aside heavy pans and trays of processed meat that have been scattered across a wide stove. A single gas ring is still lit and has cremated whatever was once in the pan on top of it. Somebody must have been here recently.

You turn off the gas and move past the serving hatch, grabbing something metal on your way. You glance down and realise that you've grabbed a rusty spatula. Its edges

have been sharpened through years of use,
but the rust on the handle means that it
might not last long. You can add it to your
WEAPONS if you choose.

RUSTY SPATULA:

Strength: +2
Durability: 5

Out of the corner of your eye, you spot
a flicker of movement. You stop in your
tracks, but there's nothing that you can
make out. Trying hard to convince yourself
that it's just a rat, you circle the restaurant
tables, looking for a way out.

The main entrance to the restaurant is on
the far side of the room. Pushing tables out
of the way, you make your way towards it.
Just as you are about to open the doors,
a slathering horde of pestilent creatures
burst through, sending you flying across the
room until you slam into a stack of chairs.
Gasping for air, you stagger to your feet.

Roll for a **RANDOM ZOMBIE ENCOUNTER.**

If you escape with your life, you flee
through the doors. Turn to **33**.

You hand over the box of **FIREWORKS** to the captain, who looks at them eagerly. "That'll do," he says with a laugh. "Welcome aboard."

If you are **INFECTED,** turn to **72**.

Otherwise, turn to **100**.

166

The air inside the shed is cool, and for a brief moment, you feel relief. Before you can make the most of the shade, your eyes adjust to the darkness, and you realise that you aren't the only person who has attempted to make the most of the secluded space.

"Don't hurt me!" the voice is small and timid but pleading.

You step closer and realise that it is a young woman, probably not out of her teens yet. She looks terrified, her eyes red-raw and puffy. You notice she has a long but shallow cut along her left forearm, dissecting a tattoo of a hummingbird. She catches you starting at it. "I caught in on a piece of metal," she explains urgently. "Let me come with you!"

To accept her request, turn to **106**.

To refuse, turn to **216**.

167

You can see the suspicion etched in the creases of her face, but she believes you. She steps aside, welcoming you on board. You climb into the main body of the boat and take a seat on one of the benches, welcoming the rest. She starts the engine and slowly eases the boat away from the dock. When she is satisfied that you are far enough away from the shore, she busies herself with a small parasol that you gladly accept. The shade from the burning sun is welcome, but you won't start to feel better until the bracing breeze of the open ocean once again caresses your skin.

The captain introduces herself and asks you what happened. If you have a **DIARY,** you are equipped to tell her what occurred last night. Congratulations, you have survived Tropic Terror, and your information could potentially save the world.

Your knowledge will inform the authorities, and they will be able to clean up the mess without causing widespread panic. There won't be medals or a parade, but you know that everything you have been through hasn't been in vain.

On the other hand, if you have no information to share, then your survival is a hollow victory. You may be walking away from the island with your life, but the virus unleashed on Tropic Terror has not been contained. Without that information, there is no saying what damage it will go on to do. Your only hope is that another survivor still on the island, or somebody brave enough to return, will be more thorough in their duty and can find out what happened before it is too late.

168

"My name is Emilia," she says. "I was hoping to find my parents, but I guess their chances aren't very good. I don't even have my mobile phone with me."

"Me neither," you add.

After sitting in silence for a while, you both

agree that it's time to head back out. The
rest has done you good and restored
3 HEALTH POINTS.

Turn to **149**.

169

As you approach the steps leading up to
the tourism centre, you realise you aren't
alone. Your ears have been registering a low
growling noise for a while, but it was almost
indistinguishable from the steady drone of
the air conditioning units. Now that you are
closer, you can see that it is coming from
a dog standing guard at the door to the
building. It looks like it has seen better days
and is showing signs of being infected by
the same virus that has ravaged the other
people on the island. One of its eyes is
missing, and its chest is nothing more than
ragged open wounds. Where it was once
covered in black fur, there is now nothing
but pale skin stretched over broken bones.
As you try to stare it down, you are aware
of others appearing from between the trees.
They don't seem inclined to attack, but they
are keenly aware of your presence.

You consider stepping back, but it has noticed you and is slowly approaching. Despite its wretched state, there is no way you would be able to outrun it, so your only option is to fight your way through.

INFECTED DOG:

Strength: 13
Health: 16

Once you have slain the beast, the others flee into the shadows. You know that they aren't gone for good, and if you return this way later, they will be back. However, for now, you are free to climb the steps to the entrance. You push open the doors and step into the wide entrance plaza. Turn to **52**.

170

Silence hangs over the boat for a few seconds before the man breaks back in. You can't work out if he believes your story or if he can sense the desperation in your voice, but he seems more willing to help. "I can send a helicopter to pick you up. Get to the roof of the tourism centre, and somebody will be there. It'll take a while, so take your time and be careful." The radio goes quiet again for a second before the man returns with an afterthought. "If you are messing me around, the bill is going to bankrupt you. You better not be another punk kid pulling my chain."

You have successfully summoned a **HELICOPTER.**

You thank him profusely, but the battery quickly dies, and you are left in silence. You take the man at his word and hope that he will come through. Turn to **173**.

171

The room is large enough to provide seating for maybe a dozen employees. Benches have been arranged in a horseshoe around a large coffee table, strewn with magazines, stained coffee cups and half-eaten sandwiches. You take a moment to check for any zombies, but thankfully, the room seems to be empty other than a corpse slumped against the far wall. It is dressed in the same uniform as the staff who welcomed you last night. You find the thought distasteful, but you know they might have useful information on them.

To try to check the body over, turn to **127**.

To explore the rest of the room, turn to **5**.

172

Worrying that you'll instantly regret your decision, you extend your hand. "Come with me if you like."

Elrond shakes it enthusiastically, transferring the orange crisp-dust onto your fingers. "You won't regret it." He swings his sword again, slicing through the rope holding the wooden light shade, which crashes to the ground and splinters. "I promise!"

Add **ELROND** to your **ALLIES.**

ELROND:

Strength: 10
Health: 16
Immunity: 5
Occupation: Radio Engineer
Special: Elrond is an eager but somewhat clumsy swordsman. Each time you roll for his strength in battle, if you roll a double, he misses the enemy and hits you. You lose **2 HEALTH POINTS** instead.

Shaking your head, you push the front door open and step out onto the path. Turn to **80**.

173

You explore the rest of the bow but find nothing of interest. Carefully, you make your way back across the mast to the stern of the ship. If you have already explored the stern in full, turn to **148**.

If you haven't explored the stern and wish to do so, turn to **63**.

If you would prefer to swim back to shore, turn to **214**.

174

You mumble a greeting loud enough to be heard but desperately trying not to be heard by anything outside. The chef looks up and smiles but says nothing in return. It would be awkward to leave now, so you enter the room. Turn to **154**.

175

The stairs lead up to the first floor but no further. The door at the top opens onto a long corridor of rooms. These are the hotel rooms where business guests usually stay - they aren't often afforded the luxury of a beach hut like you were. Most of the doors are locked, but you find one with the door ajar halfway along the corridor.

To head inside, turn to **4**.

To continue along the corridor, turn to **129**.

176

You sprint along the boardwalk until you reach the end of the jetty. Behind you, you hear the sounds of dozens of zombies racing after you. You turn around as they emerge from the trees, fighting each other for the chance to get to you.

If you have alerted a **PARTY BOAT**, turn to **193**.

If you have managed to make a call for a **RESCUE BOAT**, turn to **155**.

Otherwise, turn to **28**.

177

You follow the narrow track until it reaches a fork. To your right, the path seems to lead towards a small hut decorated with images of watersports. To head there, turn to **125**. Otherwise, the path leads straight ahead. To follow it, turn to **187**.

178

The path curves through a manicured bed filled with flowers and towering palm trees until it reaches a plaza. It branches off towards a small pool, bordered by a couple of huts. If you haven't investigated the pool before and wish to now, turn to **190**. Otherwise, you can follow the path onwards towards the beach by turning to **88**.

179

You slide the **KEY CARD** into the slot on the side of the radio, and it bursts into life. You listen to the static for a while, trying to figure out how to select a channel. Finally, you work out what does what and get started. If you know which channel to tune the radio to in order to call for help, turn to that section now. Otherwise, turn to **121**.

180

Fern pinches her lips and frowns at you. Without saying another word, she marches out of the building and disappears. You follow her to the door, but she has vanished amongst the trees. Cutting your losses, you head back out onto the path. Turn to **202**.

181

Before the man can draw his rifle, you push your heels into the sand and sprint forward. When you are a few feet away, he finally gets his hands sorted and fires a round towards you. It skims your upper arm, opening an inch-long wound that immediately burns. Remove **2 HEALTH POINTS.**

You drop to the sand and roll until your back crashes into a deckchair at the base of the barricade. You grab hold of something above you and pull yourself to your feet just as the group of tourists emerge from the small hatch. They quickly surround you and take it in turns to attack. Due to the fact that you have to fend off strikes from multiple foes, your **STRENGTH** is reduced by -2 for this fight.

Roll a die. You must kill that number of tourists before any remaining flee back into the forest. If you are successful, turn to **199**.

TRIBAL TOURIST:
Strength: 7
Health: 4

182

If you haven't been through the double doors and wish to, turn to **29**.

Otherwise, you may leave the business centre and return to the path by turning to **116**.

183

If you haven't investigated the watersports hub yet and would like to, turn to **78**.

Otherwise, you turn and follow the path through the lush vegetation. Turn to **48**.

184

The sand is soft and dry, making progress across the beach difficult. Here, you are completely exposed to the sun, and you can

feel your skin suffering. There's no shelter, so you move closer to the water until your feet are bathing in the gentle waves.

Mosquitoes buzz around your head and arms, closing in wherever you are doused in sweat. You swat them away, but they merely circle back for more. Eventually, one of them lands on you, and you recoil at the electric sensation of a small spark.

You look closer at the insects circling you and notice that they are all surrounded by their own halo of electricity. They don't even need to land on you to send a small but painful shock to your damp skin. When a few of them attack at once, the pain is overwhelming, and you have to fight the urge to drop to the sand.

It is unlikely that you will be able to kill all of the **ELECTRIC MOSQUITOES,** but if you can do enough damage, then the rest might leave you alone. These pesky insects attack in swarms, and the damage they do varies. Each time they inflict damage, roll a die and half the number, rounding up. They deliver that many points of damage.

ELECTRIC MOSQUITOES:

Strength: 9

Health: 11

If you manage to escape, turn to **140**.

185

"Is this a joke? This is an emergency line, not a prank phone call."

"No, it's not a joke. Something happened last night, and the island has been taken over." Turn to **130**.

"Sorry, I think that was somebody else on the line. I just need somebody to collect me from the island. I need to get back home as soon as possible." Turn to **13**.

186

The wooden boards creak beneath your feet, playing out their own cautionary song. You remember the same creaks from the night before when the worst thing you had to fear ahead of you was boredom and aggressive sales pitches. After a moment, you notice a harmony to the groans, a patter of sympathetic whines that might indicate somebody following you. You have

kept a firm eye behind you, on the lookout
for any zombies, but the jetty is empty
except for a handful of errant coconuts
that have dropped from the trees lining the
beach.

You carry on, aware of the echo to your
steps. You turn again, but there is nothing
there. You turn back and pick up your pace,
desperate to reach the end of the jetty and
any chance of escape. Out
of nowhere, something hard
cracks into the back of your
skull. You shake the stars from
your eyes and turn around.

The coconuts are
standing around
waiting to see what
you do. Each one is
mutated, sprouting
hairy arms and
legs. If you look
closely, the dark
whorls in the
husk could be a
pair of menacing
eyes frowning at
you. One of them has
been cracked open, and
a small pink umbrella

and a delicate orange flower have been placed inside what you can only think of as its head. Compared to the others, it looks almost pretty, as though it is dressed up for a night on the town.

You suspected that the virus might have infected the local wildlife, but for it to mutate fruit as well is something new. Their size, speed and tough outer shell mean that these are not going to be easy to destroy. You won't be able to escape, either; they seem to work as a team, and you sense they will have no issue catching you if you flee.

Roll a die. Once you have defeated that many **MUTANT COCONUTS,** you must take on the leader with the umbrella in its head.

MUTANT COCONUT:

Strength: 10
Health: 10

MUTANT COCONUT LEADER:

Strength: 12
Health: 10

If you defeat them all, you are free to continue along the jetty. Turn to **176**.

187

The path widens as it reaches the beach before the stone paving gives way to sand-strewn steps leading down to the water's edge. A wooden post, hammered into the ground, is adorned with a pair of signs. One points to the left and is marked **CAVES.** The other, which points towards the beach, is labelled **SHIPWRECK.**

To head towards the caves, turn to **163**.

To head towards the beach, turn to **98**.

188

The room is large enough to house a double bed with a large set of wardrobes on the far side. A wooden sailor's chest that has been knocked about and seems somewhat the worse for wear has been thrown into a corner.

On one side of the room, a pair of thick curtains have been drawn, letting in the merest sliver of light. You pull them back, wincing at the already bright sun, and try to shake off a pulsing headache. Rather than a set of windows, the curtains reveal a pair

of glass doors that open onto a balcony,
beyond which a steep hill plummets towards
a sandy cove.

To try to open the sailor's chest, turn to **122**.

To open the glass doors, turn to **39**.

189

You rock precariously on the mast, gripping
tightly with your thighs until the dizziness
passes and the movement stops. Eventually,
you feel confident enough to press on,
this time making sure to not look down. It
seems to take an age, but you reach the far
side and step up onto the deck at the front
of the boat. Turn to **236**.

190

Around the pool, the path is covered in
small tiles that are slippy underfoot. You
gravitate towards the edge, leaving the
pool shrouded in moving shadows cast by
the tall palms that stand guard over the
area. You try not to allow the movement to
distract you, but every twitch and flutter of
darkness sends your heart racing.

Around the pool, there are two buildings.

The closest to you is the poolside bar, open at the front and with a deep kitchen to the rear. Beyond that, there is a small, windowless shed, locked with a small padlock.

To look inside the bar, turn to **126**.

To push on towards the shed, turn to **220**.

To leave the poolside area and return to the path, turn to **71**.

191

Whatever is moving behind the hut bumps into the wall again, followed by a deep groan. Your heart speeds up, pounding against your chest, but you push on.

The room is a mess, abandoned in a hurry by whoever was here last night. You toss clothes aside and upend suitcases and bags to try to find anything that might be of use, but most of them yield nothing. Eventually, just as you are about to give up, you notice a coffee-stained notepad wedged underneath a pile of brochures on the desk. You snatch it up and skim through it.

At first glance, it appears to be the notes of a ship's captain or somebody who has a similar responsibility. It lists times and dates for the comings and goings of the main tourist boat - you notice a line for your own arrival yesterday. Next to it, there is a hastily scrawled note:

No return scheduled. Call for pickup. Channel 37. Tourism centre.

You have no idea what it means, but the noise is getting louder and closer. You shove the **NOTE** into your **PACK** and race to the door just as a creature bursts through it.

There is something familiar about the woman standing in front of you, regardless of the shedding skin, pale green complexion and bulging red eyes. It takes you a moment, but you finally recognise her as one of the other guests at the presentation last night.

You recall that she sat a few rows in front of you and seemed particularly drunk before the speaker even began. Whatever she is suffering from now is definitely not a hangover. Her grunts and groans are her only form of communication, but it doesn't take a genius to work out what she wants.

She slowly shuffles towards you, her yawning mouth snapping and drooling with every step.

DRUNKEN ZOMBIE:

Strength: 8
Health: 8

If you kill her, you manage to escape back to the path outside. Turn to **83**.

192

You step forwards into the cave, the sickening thrill of the unknown pulsing through your veins, setting your heart on edge. What little light remained at the entrance fades quickly as you descend deeper.

Each step is measured, making sure that you retain your footing on the wet, polished stone. You know that each one takes you further into the Earth's cold embrace, and yet you already know that you have come too far to head back.

As the passageways twist and turn and your sense of direction flees, the walls seem to close in. The ceiling drops lower and lower

until you are only able to crouch, but still, you persevere.

Eventually, the realisation that you are hopelessly lost dawns. You try to turn back, but every direction is the same endless night, a labyrinth of shadow and stone. You shout, but the cave swallows all sound like it has done so many before you.

Soon, time loses all meaning. Minutes blend into hours, which give way to days, and still, you search for an exit that never comes. As madness begins to settle over you like a welcome blanket, you embrace your tomb as an ancient pharaoh might once have welcomed the afterlife. Consumed by darkness forever, you lay back and accept your fate.

193

You check your watch and count back to when you alerted the boat to your position. If you have reached this point within ten minutes, turn to **74**.

If not, turn to **119**.

194

You lunge at the hermit with your weapon, cutting him down without a fight. You feel bad at your murderous rage and recoil in horror at what you have done. Lose 3 **STRENGTH POINTS.**

Shaking and distraught, you return to the cave. To explore the dark path, turn to **141**. To investigate the rock face, turn to **146**.

195

The reception area seems empty, but you don't want to hand around.

If you haven't followed the steps down into the basement and want to head there now, turn to **200**.

Otherwise, you quickly make your way to the glass doors leading back out onto the island. To your left, the path leads towards a pool area and what looks like a small food hut. To your right, it seems to curve past a row of huts and down towards the beach.

To head left, turn to **178**.

To head right, turn to **105**.

196

The rest of the room seems to be empty except for a door on the far wall. There is a glass panel, but the room beyond is dark, and you can't see much inside it.

To open the door, turn to **219**.

To head back up to the reception, turn to **113**.

197

You close the diary and explain to Fern that you need to find a way off the island. She agrees and asks if she can join you.

To accept her offer, turn to **41**.

To refuse politely, turn to **34**.

198

Cautiously, you approach the building. You try to ignore the corpse floating in the hot tub and the missing limbs.

Inside, you give the room a cursory glance, noticing a **FIRST-AID KIT** hanging by the door.

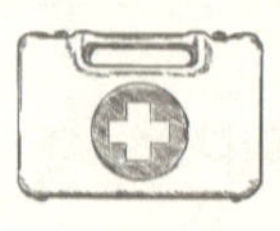

FIRST-AID KIT:
Restores health to maximum and cures **INFECTION.**

You daren't loiter for long, and you soon retreat back to the path. Turn to **110**.

199

As the last tourist falls to the sand, your heart sinks. These weren't a group of zombies hell-bent on eating you. They were scared people who just wanted to be left alone. The shame of what you've done here today grips your heart. You feel your own motivation and strength ebbing away. Reduce your **STRENGTH** by 1.

You quickly search the barricade and realise that they had precious little worth taking. Perhaps they might have been able to give you more information, but that opportunity has now passed.

Instead, you head back to the dirt track, which seems to be the only way out of the cove and return to your hut. You head through your bedroom and into the living space. Turn to **224**.

200

You quickly regret your decision as you work your way down a series of stairs that spiral into deep shadows. Occasional lights flicker and buzz but only serve to add an edge to the darkness.

When you finally reach the bottom, you can barely make out your hands in front of your face. You grope around until you find a light switch. The string snaps in your hand, but a series of lights flicker into life, illuminating a dark, concrete corridor with a pulsing glow. Turn to **69**.

201

After a short while, the path opens up into a small area bordered by benches and lush planting.

It continues ahead towards the tourism centre, but there is also a large pool nestled amongst the vegetation.

You notice a sign overhead that tells you there is a poolside bar somewhere beyond the trees.

If you haven't explored the pool and its

poolside bar before, you may do so now by turning to **190**.

Otherwise, you follow the path ahead towards the tourism centre. Turn to **231**.

202

The building soon disappears behind a row of towering palms and tree ferns, and you are once again cast into a light shade. You walk past small picnic areas and catch a glimpse of the ocean beyond the trees but nothing else of interest. The air is silent except for the soft hum of insects and the occasional cry of parrots or monkeys in the distance.

Eventually, you reach an opening in the trees that leads onto a wide grassy circle. Something stirs in the back of your mind, and you remember somebody on the boat telling you about the silent yoga sessions. He had been very eager to get you to join despite your obvious indifference.

You can enter the yoga clearing by turning to **32**.

Otherwise, you can continue along the path by turning to **225**.

203

The gravel path turns almost back on itself, heading back along the coast of the island. To your right, a wooden jetty juts out over the beach and into the water. You realise with excitement that it is where your boat docked yesterday. To head out onto the dock, turn to **186**. To continue along the path, turn to **151**.

204

The hot sand shifts beneath your feet, slipping over the tops of your shoes and burning your ankles. You press on, getting closer to the gazebo with each sluggish step. As you draw closer, you pick out the soft sound of music drifting from the far end of the wooden walkway. The two figures that you saw silhouetted seem to be moving rhythmically alongside each other, and it's only as you get closer still that you realise they are dancing slowly.

You pause halfway along the walkway to take in the full scene. A wedding is taking place, or at least it was. The guests are littering the floor of the gazebo, most of them dead, but some showing clear signs that they are about to return for another round as zombies. The two dancers are dressed better than the rest, she in a flowing white gown and he in a pale grey suit with a tropical flower pushed through his buttonhole.

Your approach hasn't gone unnoticed, and the bride and groom turn towards you, continuing their dancing embrace as they do. You see that they are fully turned, their loving gaze nothing more than the red-eyed stare of the zombies you've already met. Their flesh, once youthful and plump, now hangs ragged from their skulls. Their jaws are slack, and their nails are long and sharp.

You stand, mesmerised by the strange juxtaposition of their melancholic dancing and the horrific nature of their fate. This is a mistake, as their dancing swiftly brings them into range, and they finally part to surround you, chanting their vows over and over until the sound rings inside your head. "'Til death us do part!"

UNDEAD BRIDE:

Strength: 12
Health: 15

UNDEAD GROOM:

Strength: 13
Health: 12

If you manage to send both to their eternal peace, turn to **62**.

205

With a stomach-churning scream, you turn on your heels. You try to get your shoes to grip the damp mud. You manage to make it as far as the path, but the strange man is already upon you, barrelling into your back and knocking you to the floor. You reach out to grasp at his face, but your finger slips inside his mouth and is swiftly bitten clean off at the knuckle.

Howling with pain, you grab at your hand and stare in disbelief at the sight of your finger hanging from his mouth. Before you can react, he thrusts his head forward, sinking his teeth into the softness of your neck, and everything fades away.

A fitful sleep takes over, filled with bizarre dreams and a raging fever. When you next open your eyes, you are overcome with a sense of rage and urgency. Whatever disease had taken over your attacker now flows through your own veins. You are one of them, whatever they are.

But that's another story for another day. This one ends here with you stumbling manically through a tropical forest, seeking out any survivors.

206

The bridge looks weak, and when you step tentatively onto it, the warning groan is enough to force a retreat. If you are going to cross the bridge, you will need to make sure that you are light enough. Unfortunately, the stronger you are, the heavier your body.

Add together your **STRENGTH** and any items in your **PACK** and **WEAPONS**. If the total is greater than 16, you will need to discard some items to cross the bridge safely. Remove any items from your **PACK** or **WEAPONS** (they will be lost forever) until you are light enough.

If you would sooner avoid the bridge, you can keep your items and return to the other path by turning to **68**.

If you wish to continue across the bridge, remove your items and turn to **56**.

207

"Why did you have to escape? Sure, there's a lot of sleazy salesmen and boring hacks, I get that, but it's hardly hell on Earth."

How do you respond?

"Something went wrong last night, something bad. The island has been overrun with zombies." Turn to **185**.

"I've had bad news from home. I need to get back as quickly as possible." Turn to **13**.

208

At first, a strange smell from the fire arouses a hunger inside you. It smells sweet, like slow-roasted meat, but there is a tang of sourness to it. The closer you get, the stronger and more revolting it gets until the acrid odour of burnt hair clings to your throat. This close, you are able to make

out that the fire is burning inside an old oil drum and that the figures shuffling around it are zombies. They appear to be fighting over a large chunk of meat roasting over the flames. You try to convince yourself that it must be something they found in the island's food stores. You ignore the ponytail hanging from one end.

It doesn't look like the creatures have spotted you, so you will be able to sneak past and carry on along the path if you choose. To do so, turn to **235**.

If you would sooner turn back and follow the fork in the road, turn to **40**.

On the other hand, it looks like the path continues into the forest beyond the zombies. The business centre looms on your right, and the path seems to wind past it. To head that way, you will need to make it past the creatures. If your journey lies that way, turn to **212**.

209

Thanking the couple for what little information they have shared, you scan the cove for any other way out of there. It seems that the only escape is back along the path, so you back away until you are nestled amongst the trees again. You slowly wind your way back towards your hut, where you pass through your bedroom and enter the living space. Turn to **224**.

210

You quickly reach the next hut, the only other one in this direction. Ahead, the path terminates against the back wall of a building. There is a door, but it looks disused. The hut, meanwhile, seems to have been inhabited last night; there are a few lights on in the living space, but there doesn't seem to be any movement.

To head into the hut, turn to **55**.

To check out the door, turn to **38**.

To turn around and head back along the path in the opposite direction, turn to **145**.

211

You lower your weapon and stand up with your hands over your head like you've seen in a thousand films. Fern seems to calm down and lowers her baseball bat, although

she doesn't drop it. "What's happened here?" she asks.

If you have a **DIARY** in your **PACK,** turn to **233**.

Otherwise, turn to **87**.

212

You try to sneak past the creatures huddled around the fire, but there is nowhere to hide under the burning light of the morning sun. As soon as you step onto the path, their attention snaps away from their gruesome meal and locks onto you.

Roll for a **RANDOM ZOMBIE ENCOUNTER.**

If you survive, you continue along the path. Turn to **161**.

213

The path climbs a set of steps before dropping on the other side of a stone mound. You follow it into the chamber, which is lit by several tall, dribbling candles. Whoever lives here, and there is no doubt that somebody does, is a hoarder of other people's junk. The space is strewn with discarded rubbish, given a new life as a

treasured possession. Beyond the candles,
there are various suitcases, skulls and
a strange collection of toothbrushes. It
appears that the owner collects whatever
the tourists leave behind. There's even an
inflatable alligator hanging from the ceiling.

"Hands off!" The voice belongs to a spry
old man, naked except for a tattered pair
of Hawaiian swimming shorts, who leaps
out from behind a rock and tries to stand
between you and everything.

To attack the man, turn to **194**.

To see how it plays out, turn to **31**.

214

Almost immediately, you regret your
decision. Without the scuba equipment, you
are forced to battle against the waves that
churn on the surface of the ocean. They
aren't the kind you'd see surfers riding,
but they don't need to be. They are pulling
away from the shore, taking you with them.

No matter how much energy you exert, they
fight back with more. It doesn't take long
before you lose the battle. With a crushing

thump that knocks any remaining air from
your lungs, you are thrown back against the
hull of the boat.

You feel the pain of something sharp
cracking into your skull, and everything
slips out of focus. As the darkness
descends, so do you, doomed to become
nothing more than crab-food.

215

The building itself is built of wood, but it is
sturdy. There is no pathway around it, so
you are forced to tread through damp mud
and brush past tangled bushes and broad
palm leaves that drip water past your collar
and down your spine.

Shivering and hoping that you don't meet
any spiders, you push past them until you
reach the rear of the building. Here you find
the debris that adorns the back of every
staff building - a few rotting benches, trays
filled with cigarette butts and a pile of old
fizzy drink cans. It's strange to remember
that the staff were enjoying a quick drink
only yesterday, blisfully unaware of the
nightmare that they'd wake up to. Or not.

Like staff areas everywhere, it seems to be accessed by a fire door. You kick the rubbish out of the way and push hard against it with your shoulder. It budges but doesn't open.

Test your **STRENGTH.**

If you pass, turn to **54**.

Otherwise, turn to **79**.

216

"I'm sorry," you say firmly. "I don't know you, and you might be infected. I can't take that risk."

You ignore the girl's sobs and head back out into the sun.

To head to the gazebo, turn to **204**.

To head past the gazebo and on towards the dock, turn to **184**.

217

There must be a sensor hidden somewhere in the bushes because something beeps at your approach, and the gate in front of you silently swings open.

You make a point of closing it behind you, glancing at the notice pinned to the front:

Access to holiday rentals and caves.
Permit holders only.

It appears that you discovered an alternative way into a reserved area of the island. On the other side of the gate, the path divides.

One direction leads past a wooden hut and down towards a beach. The other direction heads back inland and seems to lead towards the glass structure of the tourism centre.

To head towards the beach, turn to **105**.

Otherwise, turn to **169**.

218

As soon as you enter the medical centre, you hear noises coming from the back rooms. You act quickly, trying to sort through the shelves of equipment for anything that might be useful. You grab two **FIRST-AID KITS** and add them to your **PACK.**

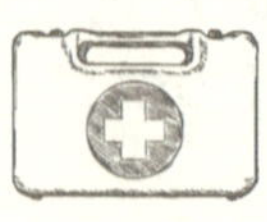

FIRST-AID KIT:
Restores health to maximum and cures **INFECTION.**

The noises are getting louder, but it looks like there might be more useful equipment in some of the other boxes. To keep looking, turn to **222**. To head back out, turn to **117**.

219

The door creaks open ominously, filling the space with noise that echoes and drills into your ears. You step into the room, feeling for a light switch and bathing it in a weak green light. On the far wall, a bank of electronic equipment fills every square inch. In the centre of it, there is a radio.

If you have a **KEY CARD,** turn to **179**.
If you have **ELROND** as an **ALLY,** turn to **150**.
Otherwise, turn to **60**.

220

The small lock on the shed door doesn't last long, succumbing to your second kick. You yank the door open, ready to attack whatever is inside, and are mildly disappointed to find it devoid of any

monsters. Instead, you discover a well-maintained chainsaw hanging from a hook on the wall. It's a bulky piece of equipment, and you will struggle to carry any other weapons with it. If you choose to take the **CHAINSAW,** you must discard any other weapons you are holding and may not pick up any more until you drop the chainsaw. If you have any allies, you may pass on a single weapon to each of them before discarding the rest.

CHAINSAW:

Strength: +5
Durability: 20

Once you have decided, you leave the shed and return to the poolside area. If you haven't already been into the poolside bar and wish to investigate, turn to **126**. If you have, or you would prefer to return to the path, turn to **162**.

221

There is a strange smell rising from the burning barrel, almost sweet with a strong sour undertone. You draw closer, trying to work out what is being cooked. As you approach, the shadowy figures shuffling around it come into focus, and you realise that they are a small pack of zombies. Whatever they are cooking, you don't want to know, especially as the smell becomes more acrid the closer you get. It will be possible to avoid them and head towards a fork in the main path just beyond. To do so, turn to **15**. However, there is another path that lies beyond the burning barrel. Sneaking that way will be much more difficult, but it appears to lead past the business centre towards the ocean. To attempt to sneak past the fire, turn to **212**.

222

Frustration burns the back of your eyes as each box yields nothing more than old paperwork and stale biscuits. In anger, you throw one to the ground, where it slides across the floor and smashes an ornate vase. The sound echoes against the clinical, white walls and is returned with a loud groan from the next room. Before you can flee, an old man shuffles in, his white doctor's coat smeared with gore. At first, you think his jaw is hanging open, but then you realise that the entire lower part is missing; his tongue flaps freely whenever he judders towards you.

As soon as he notices you, his pace quickens, and he is on top of you before you react. You wrestle out from underneath him, managing to keep your arms clear of his upper molars. Once you are free, you steady yourself for the fight.

OLD ZOMBIE DOCTOR:

Strength: 7
Health: 6

If you defeat him, turn to **115**.

223

The beach is littered with detritus cast aside by the tide. You pick through it with your toes as you progress across the sand. There isn't much of interest, although you do unearth a **TORCH**. If you don't already have one in your **PACK**, you may add this one.

You make a point of sticking close to the treeline as you head back across the beach, not wanting to encounter another mutated crocodile. It doesn't matter where you walk;

everywhere is shrouded in an ominous tension that keeps your nerves buzzing. It is only this adrenalin that allows you to react quickly when something bursts from the trees. You retreat from its hideous form, humanoid but covered in fleshy green strands and smelling overwhelmingly of salt and fish. As the strange apparition lurches towards you, you try not to scream or vomit. It sheds bits of its strange skin with each step, and eventually, you realise that you are looking at a lich.

After years of reading stories and listening to your nerdy sister talk about her roleplay games, you are well aware of the undead spellcasters known as liches. Drawn from the realms of the dead by a form of dark magic, they have only ever appeared in fantasy tales until now. Whatever has been unleashed on the island is clearly doing more than turning people into zombies. First, crocodiles glowing with radiation, and now this?

Luckily for you, the seaweed-covered lich doesn't appear to have any magical powers. However, it is still a ferocious enemy

powered by the strength of the dead and almost unkillable.

Your only hope is the creature's slow speed. If you are able to slip past its embrace, you will be able to flee to safety. At the beginning of each round, roll a die. On a 6, you are able to escape. Turn to **234**.

Until then, you must fight the monster as normal.

SEAWEED LICH:

Strength: 15
Health: 45

224

As you enter the room, your presence wakes the small man sleeping on the couch. He rolls over with a loud yawn, misjudging the width of the sofa and crashing to the wooden floor with a painful thud. He swears and leaps to his feet, wincing and grabbing his lower back. For the first time, he glances in your direction and startles backwards, his hand landing in a bowl of orange crisps, evidence of a late-night snack.

"Elrond Smythe," he grumbles, extending a

hand coated in orange dust.

"Elrond?" you ask, trying to avoid shaking.

"My mum was a bit of a nerd," he says with a chuckle, finally lowering his hand and wiping the crumbs onto his trousers. "What time is it?"

You haphazardly point in the direction of the clock, trying to look around the rest of the room. "Oof, I overslept," he says. You hear him grab another handful from the bowl and stuff it into his mouth. "What did I miss?" he adds, spraying crumbs.

If you have information to share, turn to **64**.

Otherwise, turn to **160**.

225

Eventually, the path ends and diverges in separate directions. Looking left, you see that it ends at a wooden pier, which you immediately recognise as the one on which you landed last night.

To your right, the path leads away into thick strands of palms and artfully placed white boulders.

If you have already been to the pier and wish to return, turn to **176**.

If you haven't visited the pier and wish to head there now, turn to **186**.

Otherwise, you follow the path away from the beach. Turn to **201**.

226

To follow the path through the lush vegetation, turn to **48**.

To head south towards the tourism centre, turn to **36**.

227

The man mumbles something under his breath, and the radio clicks into silence. You frantically try to regain contact but to no avail. Eventually, the battery dies, and you give up. Turn to **173**.

228

"I'm not going to do that," you argue. "I don't know if you're still going to attack me. Let's talk about this."

If you have a **DIARY** in your **PACK**, turn to **233**.

Otherwise, turn to **114**.

229

After a few moments, the vent forks. It is too dark to really see anything, although a few shafts of flickering light add a soft glow to the passage to your right. There is also a rapid humming noise coming from that direction. Where the metal tunnel carries on ahead, it is dark and silent.

To head onwards, turn to **95**.

To turn right, turn to **58**.

230

The captain listens intently whilst you describe the chaos on the island and the mystery of last night. She pauses for a beat before hissing, "I bloody knew there was something weird about those scientists."

You wait for her to finish arguing with somebody in the background before she returns to the radio. "I'll come and get you. Get to the dock as quickly as you can. I'll wait off the coast until I see you, and then I'll haul ass to get you. I'm not hanging around too close to the island."

You have called for a **RESCUE BOAT**.

You thank her profusely, and the radio crackles into silence. The only other item of interest in the room is a heavy wrench.

WRENCH:

Strength: +2
Durability: Unlimited
Special: The wrench is heavy. For the first attack with this weapon in each battle, only roll a single die for your attack.

You leave the room and head back out into the basement. Ahead of you, there is a set of elevator doors that are marked for the roof of the building. Next to them, a set of stairs leads back up to the main reception area.

To take the elevator to the roof, turn to **43**.

To take the stairs, turn to **195**.

You wander cautiously along the path, enclosed on one side by the crystal iceberg of the tourism centre and on the other, beyond the lines of palm trees, the sound of the beach. Ahead of you, you can make out a low growling sound, but from where you are walking, you can't see any signs of a potential attacker. You push on more slowly, keeping your wits about you. When you turn a corner and reach the steps up to the entrance of the tourism centre, you see the source of the noise.

At the foot of the steps, a dog limps in a circle. Judging by the ragged flesh on its chest and torn ears, it appears to have been attacked. It notices you but stays where it is, trying desperately to lick its wounds. The only way into the building lies past the dog, so you will need to approach it if you wish to go that way. The path you are on also continues beyond the dog. Alternatively, there is a track through the trees to your left. It doesn't appear to be an official path; instead, it's nothing more than a trampled area where previous tourists cut through to reach the beach.

To head past the dog and into the building, turn to **10**.

To avoid the dog and cut through the trees, turn to **59**.

232

You approach the water cautiously. Up close, it smells rancid, and the dark red hue of the blood clouds the water. The surface is still undisturbed, but for the occasional bubble that rises to the surface, never in the same place twice. You lean in, careful not to dip your toes in the water.

The water erupts in front of you, a flayed mess of flesh and bones rising up like Poseidon. It leaps from the water like a graceless dolphin; you stagger back just in time as the hulking mass splats down onto the edge of the pool with a sad, wet sound. The bloated corpse of a man turns its head slowly, fixing a single yellow eye on you. It moves its mouth as if to speak, but only bubbles appear.

Slowly, the corpse pushes itself to its feet, one swollen and blistered, the other nothing more than bone and tendon, and staggers

towards you. The effects of the water have swollen the body to twice its normal size, and the man wasn't small to begin with. His tongue, fat and limp, hangs from his mouth like an eager dog.

It lurches towards you, bloody water dripping onto the ground.

BLOATED CORPSE:
Strength: 11
Health: 6

If you manage to send the corpse sprawling back to whatever hell spawned it, you turn and head back along the path towards the trees. Turn to **23**.

233

You open the diary to the next passage and begin to read it out loud.

We confirmed with Henrik Flagstaff that his seminar was going to be strictly informational in the weeks leading up to the event. His position didn't change; he wanted to demonstrate the power of his new virus in a controlled manner, and we shouldn't be acting as a barrier to stop him. My own bosses begged him to reconsider and even threatened to ban his appearance altogether, but his company had pumped so much money into the resort that they had no choice.

In the end, I suppose they hoped that he would change his mind when he arrived or that his "experiment" could be contained. I don't think any of us saw it becoming the disaster that it did.

"Is there any more information?" Fern asks.

To keep reading, turn to **86**.

If you'd sooner leave the diary until later, turn to **197**.

234

Ignoring the howls of the strange monster, you flee across the sand until you are lost in the dense understory of palm trees and ferns. You know that the caves lie this way, so you press on until you discover a waterfall cascading into an open pool that itself feeds the ocean a few yards away.

Behind the waterfall, you find the entrance to a dark cave. You enter cautiously.

Turn to **134**.

235

There is a small building by the side of the path. A sign on the front marks it out as a medical centre. The door is shut, but there is no telling whether it is locked. There are a few lights on inside the building, but no sign of movement. Next to the medical centre is another building. It looks like a hut similar to the one that you spent the night in. The door is open, and the lights are on, but it seems equally silent.

To head into the medical centre, turn to **218**.

To look inside the hut, turn to **16**.

236

The bow of the ship is smaller than the stern, and there isn't much to explore. You search through the wooden crates, most of which are rotten and empty, before moving on to the more modern metal case. It is closed with a watertight catch but unlocked.

You flick the catch and swing open the lid, shouting with delight at what you find. Inside, you discover a long-range communication radio. You push the switch,

and it buzzes into life, crackling with static
and humming gently.

You cycle through the channels, shouting
for help until you finally hear a response. It
is broken and weak, but you can just about
make out what they are saying.

"This is Jefferson Airfield, the only airfield in
the archipelago. This is an emergency line.
How can I help?"

How do you respond?

"There's been an outbreak of zombies, and I
need rescuing." Turn to **185**.

"I've managed to get stuck on an old boat
and need somebody to pick me up."

Turn to **11**.

237

The path opens up until it forms a wide
junction, heading off in two separate
directions.

To the south, it appears to pass by the tall
glass structure of the tourism centre.

To the east, the path curves away, heading

towards more huts. In the distance, you can just make out the business centre where you vaguely remember spending part of last night. Closer, you can see the flickering light of a small fire, possibly a bonfire.

To head south, turn to **65**.

To head east, turn to **90**.

TURN THE PAGE FOR THE

RANDOM ZOMBIE ENCOUNTERS TABLE

RANDOM ZOMBIE ENCOUNTERS

WHO WILL YOU FIGHT?
ROLL A DIE...

1   HALF-TURNED ZOMBIE

STRENGTH: 6

HEALTH: 5

SPECIAL: If you roll a double on any of your attacks, the part of the zombie that hasn't turned yet recognises the horror around them. They flee in terror.

2   DRIBBLING WRECK

STRENGTH: 8

HEALTH: 6

SPECIAL: None. They are wretched shells of their former self, doing nothing but dribble and bite.

3   OUTRIGHT TERROR

STRENGTH: 12

HEALTH: 15

SPECIAL: These beasts instil terror in any living creature. If they win two rounds in a row, their damage output increases to **3 HEALTH POINTS.**

4 LIMBLESS HORROR

STRENGTH: 11

HEALTH: 16

SPECIAL: There is little left of these poor creatures other than their body. They only inflict **1 HEALTH POINT** damage each time they attack.

5 LUCKY DUCK

Any creatures in your vicinity are spooked by something and flee immediately. It might be your heroic pose or a strange sound in the distance, but you avoid any conflict...this time.

6 ABHORRENT GHOUL

STRENGTH: 17

HEALTH: 20

SPECIAL: What else do they need? They are strong and take a lot of killing. You only ever fight one **ABHORRENT GHOUL** at a time, so you don't need to roll the second die to determine how many to fight.

IF YOU LOVE FANTASY...

If you love well-crafted worlds and epic fantasy adventures, you will enjoy Matt Beighton's Shadowland Chronicles.

When Trixie Grimble finds herself trapped on a distant world and embroiled in the middle of a dark and ancient war, she has to decide what she is prepared to do to make it back home.

Available online and at all good bookstores.

ABOUT THE AUTHOR

Matt Beighton is a full-time writer, born somewhere in the midlands in England during the heady days of the 1980s. He is happily married with two young daughters who keep him very busy and suffer through the endless early drafts of his stories.

Matt's books have been read around the world and awarded the LoveReading4Kids "Indie Books We Love" and Readers' Favorite 5 Star Awards.

Having spent many years as a primary-school teacher, Matt Beighton knows how to bring stories to life. He regularly visits schools and runs creative workshops that ignite a passion for words.

If you have enjoyed reading this book, please leave a review online. Your words really do keep us going!

To find out more visit

www.mattbeighton.co.uk